Murder at the Witching Hour

by

Kathi Daley

This book is a work of fiction. Names, characters, places, and incidents either are products of the author's imagination or are used fictitiously. Any resemblance to actual events or locales or persons, living or dead, is entirely coincidental.

I want to thank the very talented Jessica Fischer for the cover art.

I so appreciate Bruce Curran, who is always ready and willing to answer my cyber questions.

And, of course, thanks to the readers and bloggers in my life, who make doing what I do possible.

Thank you to Randy Ladenheim-Gil for the editing.

Special thanks to Jeanie Daniel, Nancy Farris, Pam Curran, and Joanne Kocourek for submitting recipes.

And finally I want to thank my sister Christy for always lending an ear and my husband Ken for allowing me time to write by taking care of everything else.

Books by Kathi Daley

Come for the murder, stay for the romance.

Zoe Donovan Cozy Mystery:

Halloween Hijinks
The Trouble With Turkeys
Christmas Crazy
Cupid's Curse
Big Bunny Bump-off
Beach Blanket Barbie
Maui Madness
Derby Divas
Haunted Hamlet
Turkeys, Tuxes, and Tabbies
Christmas Cozy
Alaskan Alliance
Matrimony Meltdown
Soul Surrender
Heavenly Honeymoon
Hopscotch Homicide
Ghostly Graveyard
Santa Sleuth
Shamrock Shenanigans
Kitten Kaboodle
Costume Catastrophe
Candy Cane Caper – *October 2016*

Tj Jensen Paradise Lake Mysteries

Coming September 6, 2016, from Henery Press

Pumpkins in Paradise
Snowmen in Paradise
Bikinis in Paradise
Christmas in Paradise
Puppies in Paradise
Halloween in Paradise
Treasure in Paradise – *April 2017*

Whales and Tails Cozy Mystery:

Romeow and Juliet
The Mad Catter
Grimm's Furry Tail
Much Ado About Felines
Legend of Tabby Hollow
Cat of Christmas Past
A Tale of Two Tabbies
The Great Catsby
Count Catula – *September 2016*
Cat of Christmas Present – *November 2016*

Seacliff High Mystery:

The Secret
The Curse
The Relic
The Conspiracy
The Grudge

Sand and Sea Hawaiian Mystery:

Murder at Dolphin Bay
Murder at Sunrise Beach
Murder at the Witching Hour

Road to Christmas Romance:

Road to Christmas Past

Cast - (In addition to Luke, Lani, Cam, and Kekoa)

Ivan – groom
Morticia (Tisha) – bride
Buck – Ivan's brother
Bunny – Buck's wife
Crystal – Tisha's sister
Cory – Crystal's date
Lazarus – Ivan's best friend
Lilith – Lazarus's date
Drusilla – Morticia's best friend
Damien – Drusilla's date
Cole – Ivan's friend
Raven – Cole's date

Also on island:
Dharma – psychic
Oz – priest
Mr. Graves – groundskeeper
Mrs. Baker – cook
blind butler

Chapter 1

Friday, October 28

When my friend Tisha asked me to attend her wedding I knew it would most likely be an original and somewhat eccentric affair. You see, she has an odd personality. Please understand that I don't mean that in a mean or disrespectful way. Tisha is actually a very sweet person despite the fact that she tends to redefine herself every few years by immersing herself in the fad of the moment.

After graduating high school at the top of our class, she turned down all the colleges that had accepted her and tossed her education aside in favor of moving to a commune with a group of throwbacks to the sixties' hippie movement. At some point during her tenure at the commune she met an artist, and the next thing I knew, she'd sold all her worldly goods, which wasn't a lot by that point, moved to Paris, and embraced the starving artist lifestyle. When I saw her a year ago she was back in Hawaii living in a convent, with plans to become a nun, but when I ran into her just a few weeks ago she'd dyed her blond hair black, changed her name from Patricia to Morticia, and traded her habit for piercings, tattoos, and black leather from head to foot. I realize Tisha has always been searching for a sense of identity, and I even support her desire to try to find herself, but in my opinion she's taken her interest in the *other worldly* and *undead* to a whole new level.

My cousin, roommate, and best friend Kekoa, who likewise knew Tisha from high school, was also asked to attend the somewhat wacky wedding. We were each allowed to bring a guest, so I asked my boyfriend, Luke Austin. We'd been casually dating for the past few months and, while we'd yet to make the move toward complete intimacy, I had the feeling it was only a matter of time. Luke seemed as content to keep things casual as I had indicated I'd prefer our relationship to remain, but there were times I'd look into his eyes and see a heat that didn't belong in the casual dating zone.

Kekoa wasn't currently dating anyone so she had asked our roommate, Cameron Carrington, to be her plus-one. In all there were four of us, along with six others, who stood waiting at the dock to board the boat that would take us to the private island where the four-day event was to take place.

"I have to hand it to you, Lani Pope; you have an interesting group of friends," Cam whispered to me as he took in the guests waiting for a ride.

"They aren't really my friends; they're friends of Tisha and her fiancé, although those I have had the opportunity to meet are generally pretty nice despite their choice of attire."

"So fill me in," Cam urged. "Who's who exactly?"

Luke, who was dressed in tight jeans and a sky blue T-shirt that brought out the color in his eyes, was chatting with three other men. One was tall and thin with purple hair and multiple tattoos and piercings. Another was dressed in tight jeans, a plaid shirt, and cowboy boots, and the third looked like a surfer headed for the beach.

"I believe the man in the cowboy garb is named Buck," I informed Cam. "I haven't met him, but Tisha mentioned that Ivan's Texas cowboy brother would be attending the affair, so by the process of elimination, I'm going to guess the man Luke is talking to is the brother Tisha mentioned. I'm also going to guess the brunette dressed like a housewife from the fifties is his wife, Bunny."

"Ivan is the groom?"

"Yes. Tisha said the brothers are really different and don't even know each other well, but Tisha believes it's bad luck to start a marriage without the blessing of the whole family, so she felt it was important that he be included in the wedding party."

"Makes sense. So, is Buck an actual cowboy or is that just his role for this little shindig?" Cam wondered.

"Tisha said he owns a ranch in East Texas. A big one. I guess, like his brother, he's quite well off."

"And did Ivan, who I assume based on the wedding theme is into the whole Goth thing, grow up in Texas?"

"No. According to Tisha, Ivan's parents divorced when he was young and his mother took him and moved to Los Angeles. Buck, who's quite a bit older than Ivan, stayed behind with his father. Tisha said their parents really, really hated each other, so they rarely arranged for visits between the two brothers. When Tisha found out about Ivan's estrangement from his brother she went behind Ivan's back and invited Buck to the wedding."

"Does Ivan know his brother and sister-in-law are going to be there?"

"He does now. Tisha told me that she decided to come clean to avoid an awkward meeting when we all arrived on the island."

Cam whistled and raised his eyebrows. "Suddenly this weird party just got a whole lot more interesting."

"I know you're hoping for a soap-opera-type drama, but for Tisha's sake let's hope the brothers get along and fireworks can be avoided."

To be perfectly honest, the more I found out about the strange affair, the more concerned I was that a soap-opera-type drama was exactly what we'd signed up for. When Tisha first asked me to attend her wedding I'd accepted without really thinking things through, but the more I got to know about Tisha's current lifestyle, the more I began to regret my promise to attend.

Cam turned and looked directly at me. "So what about Tisha's family? Are they attending this circus as well?"

I nodded. "The woman Kekoa is talking to with the long auburn hair wearing the denim cutoffs and halter top is Tisha's half sister, Crystal. She's Tisha's only family now that her mother passed away. They shared a father, who was killed in an auto accident five years ago. Crystal is a couple of years younger than Tisha, but it seems they get along okay. I noticed she arrived at the dock with the blond man wearing the board shorts and the white tank, so I'm assuming he's her boyfriend. I've never met him, but Tisha told me her sister was bringing a date named Cory who's into surfing and hiking."

"Are Crystal and Cory into the whole Goth thing too?"

"No. I think they're more into the beach thing. I chatted with Crystal when we went shopping with Tisha for a wedding dress last week, and while we didn't talk all that much about our lives outside the wedding, I got the impression she's only tolerating her sister's strange new obsession. In fact, she seemed somewhat worried about the whole thing."

"Based on what you've told me about the frequency with which your friend changes her personality, I think Crystal could be justified in her concern."

I frowned. "Yeah. I see your point."

I glanced toward Crystal, who was laughing at something Kekoa had said. She didn't look overly concerned about her sister's future, so maybe she'd spoken to Tisha since the shopping trip and they'd worked everything out.

"And the others?" Cam asked. "Based on the overuse of black despite the heat I'm going to guess that like the bride and groom, the whole group is firmly entrenched in the world of Goth?"

"I believe they are. I'm not sure of the level of commitment the others have for the dark lifestyle, but Tisha's fiancé wanted to get married on Halloween, and the wedding *is* going to take place on the Day of the Dead, so Tisha decided she'd embrace his wish and go with a Halloween theme. Tisha's wedding dress is long, tight, and black. She's wearing a black veil over her face so she looks like a widow in mourning."

"Okay, that's weird."

"Yeah, I guess it is. Like I said, Tisha has an odd way about her."

"Is the groom going to dress up as a corpse?" Cam wondered with a grin.

"No. Tisha mentioned that Ivan is fascinated with Dracula, so I guess he'll be dressed as Dracula. All the guests have been asked to dress up as well. I think Kekoa plans for you to dress up as a zombie."

Cam chuckled. "When Kekoa texted while I was visiting my parents and asked if I would be her plus-one at her friend's wedding I had no idea I was going to have to die in order to attend the affair."

"I don't think anyone is going to actually die, and dressing up could be fun. After all, it *is* Halloween. Besides, I hear the island we're being whisked off to is really spectacular. Tisha showed me a few photos of the place. The house is really a castle that was designed to look like Dracula's, which I'll admit is a bit odd for Hawaii, but Tisha has assured me that no expense has been spared to make sure everyone has a wonderful time. I'm pretty sure the food alone is going to make the weekend worth the trip."

"I know you said you and Kekoa met Morticia in high school, but I went to the same school and I don't remember anyone with that name."

"That's because Morticia is actually named Patricia. She changed her name to complement her lifestyle."

"Patricia?" Cam still looked confused.

"Patricia Cromwell."

He frowned. "Patricia Cromwell the straight-A student who attended study hall for fun whether she had homework to do or not?"

"That's her. Obviously she's changed quite a bit since then."

"I guess so. I'm having a hard time picturing Patricia as a Goth queen. I remember her as being somewhat mousy. Supersmart with absolutely no social skills. She wore those thick glasses and had braces until her senior year. Didn't she hang with the drama crowd?"

"For a while. She tended to hop around from group to group, looking for a place to land. Thinking about it, it doesn't seem she ever did find the sense of community she was looking for."

Cam shook his head. I didn't blame him if the entire setup for our weekend was blowing his mind. It had blown mine at first too, but I guess enough time had passed that I'd begun to accept the strange situation for what it was. Cam had been out of town and had just returned the previous evening, so he was just being introduced to the facts surrounding the event for the first time.

"You realize this whole thing is ridiculous," Cam stated.

"I know. But Tisha is a friend, although admittedly not a close friend. Still, she asked me to attend her wedding and I decided on the spur of the moment to do so."

"I guess it won't be boring." Cam looked toward the dock, where a woman with long blond hair and leather pants stood alone. "What about her? What's her deal?"

"Her name is Drusilla. She's Tisha's best friend, or at least that's the way Tisha introduced her when I ran into them a few weeks ago. To be honest, I didn't pick up on a best friend vibe."

"What do you mean?"

I shrugged. "I don't know. For one thing, in my mind best friends should be comfortable with each other. They should know each other well and be able to anticipate their moods and thoughts to a certain degree. When Tisha introduced me to Drusilla she seemed awkward and unsure of herself."

"Maybe Drusilla just doesn't like to meet new people, which made Tisha uncomfortable introducing her."

"Maybe, but I sensed something more. After we chatted for a while Tisha told me she was engaged and invited me to the wedding. She turned and glanced at Drusilla as if to gauge her reaction. Drusilla frowned and Tisha averted her eyes. The whole thing seemed weird, but a few seconds later Drusilla seconded the invitation by saying something like, *yes, you have to come.* I hesitated for a few seconds, but the look in Tisha's eyes seemed to me to be one of desperation. I eventually agreed to attend, and after that Tisha asked me to bring Kekoa along as well."

"And you've spoken to them since that time?"

"Yes. Tisha, Drusilla, Crystal, Kekoa, and I all went shopping together. We actually had a really good time. Drusilla definitely has a taciturn personality, which I could see Tisha was trying desperately to mimic, but Crystal was funny and outgoing, and even Dru, as I eventually began to refer to her, seemed to lighten up as the day progressed. Once Dru began to relax Tisha did too, and we managed to have several meaningful conversations."

"Which is how you know the down low on everyone, including their background?"

"Exactly. Tisha became quite chatty by the end of the day."

"So how many people are attending this four-day affair?" Cam asked.

"I'm not really sure."

I watched as Kekoa broke away from the conversation she was having with Crystal and headed toward where Cam and I were standing. She had a frown on her face and an expression that seemed to indicate that she had something serious on her mind.

"Crystal seems to be in a better mood today than she was during the shopping trip," I commented.

"Maybe." Kekoa glanced in her direction. Cory had joined Crystal after Kekoa walked away and they seemed to be involved in a serious conversation. "Crystal was smiling and seemed like she was trying to put on a happy front, but I picked up a weird vibe."

"Weird vibe?" I asked.

"Her smile seemed forced. The entire time I was talking to her I had this strange feeling that there was more going on that it might seem on the surface. It might be nothing. I just hope I don't regret using most of my vacation days to attend this wedding." Kekoa sighed.

Kekoa and I both worked at the Dolphin Bay Resort. I worked as a lifeguard and Kekoa worked the front desk of the hotel. I normally had Thursdays, Sundays, and Mondays off, so I only had to use two vacation days, but Kekoa was currently on a schedule that included having Tuesday and Wednesday off, so she'd needed to take four vacation days in all.

"I know how you're feeling." I glanced at the eclectic group that had gathered to wait for the boat. "I've had the same thought more than once since getting the down low on everyone during the shopping trip, but we already took the time off and committed to attend, so I say we make the best of it."

"You're right," Kekoa visibly relaxed. "It's not like I can afford to take a real vacation with my time off anyway."

"It looks like the boat is coming. I'm going to grab Luke to help load all this luggage."

Chapter 2

When the ten of us arrived on the island we were greeted by a man dressed as an undertaker. I later found out he was the groundskeeper, Mr. Graves, who had been commissioned to drive a small black minibus made to look like a hearse from the dock to the house. The island was large for a private one in Hawaii, and the house was located in the center. It was impossible to gauge the island's size without taking a look around. The terrain was covered in the dense foliage that thrived in this tropical climate. Large shrubs featuring colorful flowers lined the narrow path that had been paved for use by the island's vehicles. Mr. Graves pointed to a trail that disappeared into the jungle, assuring us that if we were up for a hike the spectacular view and a long waterfall were worth the effort to see.

When we arrived at the house Mr. Graves unloaded our luggage, while a man dressed as a butler who appeared to be blind—though I assumed that was an act— escorted us to our rooms. Kekoa and I shared a room on the third floor, while Luke and Cam each had been provided their own rooms on the same floor. Buck and Bunny and Crystal and Cory were on the second floor, and I noticed Drusilla and Damien had continued farther down the hall toward a closed door I assumed led to a separate wing or perhaps stairs to another level.

There were six bedrooms on the third floor and I found myself wondering who had been assigned to the other three. Tisha had told me in a previous conversation that she and Ivan shared a suite at the very top of the house, and I knew there were at least four other people staying in the house in addition to the ten of us from the boat.

"Can you believe this house?" Kekoa asked as she jumped onto one of the two queen-size beds in the large but dark room. It looked like Kekoa had decided to embrace the weekend rather than fretting about her decision to attend once she'd gotten a look at the place.

"It really is spectacular," I agreed. "When Tisha told me she was marrying a rich man I guess I pictured regular rich, not Richie Rich rich. I knew he owned a private island and the photos of the house were pretty grand, but the actual castle is, wow. I wonder how many rooms this place has. It looks like a freaking palace from the outside."

"Tisha said the house has its own theater, an atrium, and a fully equipped gym. I hope we have the chance to look around."

"Me too, although, the décor of the castle makes me feel like I'm in one of those movies where everyone dies except one person who, in the end, has a look of horror on his face as the movie ends, so you never really know whether he made it out or not. I mean, what's up with all the black curtains? There are probably hundreds of windows in the house, but every single one of them is covered to prevent the light from coming in. You don't think Ivan really is a vampire, do you?"

"Of course not." Kekoa rolled her eyes. "I'm sure he's just role-playing, the same as Tisha. I have to admit I had my doubts about the weekend, but these rooms are nicer than the suites at the Dolphin Bay. Did you see the Jacuzzi in the bathroom? And these sheets. These are not inexpensive sheets."

"The rooms are nice. Very nice. And the grounds are spectacular, but still... Did you catch the chains on the wall as we made our way up the staircase between the second and third floor?"

"I'm sure they were hung for decorative purposes only," Kekoa assured me. "What are you thinking of wearing to the welcome dinner this evening?"

I looked down at the shorts and tank top I had on. "This?"

"You can't wear that. Tisha never specifically said what attire was appropriate for the weekend, but I can only assume that if the host is planning a formal dinner we should dress in something other than faded shorts. Did you bring any dresses?"

"A dress for the wedding and a dress for the rehearsal dinner."

"I brought a few different sun dresses. You can wear one tonight."

Four days of having to dress up didn't sound like my kind of fun. Living at the beach and being a lifeguard, my normal attire consisted of bathing suits, shorts, tank tops, flip-flops, and tennis shoes, which happened to be the type of wardrobe I preferred.

I glanced at the clock on the bedside table. "We have three hours until dinner. Do you want to see if we can track down Tisha to let her know we're here?"

"I overheard Crystal ask the butler if she could see her sister when we first arrived and she was told both Morticia and Ivan preferred to remain in isolation until dinner," Kekoa informed me.

"That's strange. You'd think they would have greeted us at the dock or at least at the front door when we got here."

Kekoa shrugged. "I guess they want to make an entrance."

"Whatever. Do you want to check out the pool?"

"I'm not sure I want to swim, but I'd love to take a look at the garden. When we arrived I noticed there was both an indoor and outdoor area. If you want to take a walk with me I'll sit by the pool while you swim."

"Sounds like a plan. Should we call the guys?"

"No cell service on the island," Kekoa reminded me.

"Oh, yeah. It's going to be strange not to have it. I wonder how Ivan communicates with the outside world."

"He most likely has one of those satellite phones. We'll just stop by to tell the guys to meet us at the pool on our way down."

After slipping my bikini on under my clothes Kekoa and I entered the hallway leading from our room to the stairs. As we passed the room directly across from ours we heard voices raised in discord.

"You promised me that she wasn't going to be here," a female voice yelled. There was a loud crash that sounded like something being thrown either onto the floor or at the wall.

"I didn't think she'd show after what happened the last time we all got together," a male voice defended himself.

"You know how her presence sets me off."

"I know. I'll get rid of her. Just stay in the room until I can figure something out."

"As long as you're at it, get rid of the idiot she came with too."

"I can't do that. You know Ivan wants him here. Can't you just relax and go with the flow for once?"

The man's question was followed by another crash. Kekoa and I glanced at each other. We could hear a door slam from behind the closed door of the room. I assumed that must be the one leading to the private bath. A tall, dark-haired man with broad shoulders emerged from the room just as Kekoa and I started down the stairs. He was dressed all in black, which accentuated the paleness of his skin. His black eyes momentarily turned in our direction, but he didn't say anything before he went down the stairs ahead of us and across the entry.

"Do you know who's staying in that room?" I asked Kekoa after he exited the castle through the front door.

"I have no idea. I didn't recognize him."

"Yeah, me neither. I guess we can ask Tisha when we see her. In the meantime, let's head out to the garden through the back door. I have a feeling it might be a good idea to stay out of his way."

The gardens were as spectacular as the house, although, like it, they were different from any I'd ever seen. There were flowers in shades of dark red and purple, some so dark they appeared to be black. There was a stone walkway that meandered through the perfectly groomed flowerbeds, as well as several water features that seemed to add warmth to the area.

"Check out these black lilies," Kekoa gasped as she knelt down to take a closer look at the flowers. "They're really amazing."

I knelt down next to her. I wasn't really the sort of person to be fascinated by flowers, but this particular garden had a spooky feel I found quite inviting. "They're very pretty. I like these the best."

"Those are bat flowers," Kekoa informed me.

"Awesome. I feel like I'm in Dracula's garden."

Kekoa leaned back on her heels and looked around. "It does have that sort of feel to it, and the house was designed to replicate Dracula's castle, so I guess technically this *is* Dracula's garden. I love these purple nightshades. I wonder what used to be planted next to them."

I frowned. There was an area that was comprised of maybe four square feet that was devoid of plants. The soil was healthy and looked like it had recently been worked, so I had to assume someone had intentionally removed whatever had been planted there before. "The groundskeeper must be changing things up a bit."

"Perhaps. I wonder what sort of plants are inside the greenhouse."

"How about we check it out tomorrow and head over to the pool now? The garden is amazing, but it's hot. I could use a dip."

"It is hot. And muggy." Kekoa glanced toward the horizon. "It looks like a storm is coming."

I looked off into the distance as huge dark clouds made their way in our direction. The wind had picked up a bit and the air had begun to cool, but not enough to make it comfortable to be outdoors. Based on the feel of things, it looked like we were in for more than just a spot of rain, which in my opinion could be a good thing. "Those clouds do look nasty, but I heard the man who piloted the boat that brought us to the island tell Buck that the storm wasn't expected to hit until well after midnight. He did indicate that once it arrived it was going to be a big one, but I think I have time for a quick dip."

When Kekoa and I arrived at the pool we noticed the tall, dark man who was staying in the room across from us heading down the path that led to the beach. He appeared to be alone and deep in thought. I was certain he hadn't noticed us because he didn't pause to say anything or even turn his head.

"Let's follow him," I suggested.

"Why?" Kekoa asked.

"I don't know. I guess I'm just curious where he's going."

"The guys are going to meet us here any moment," Kekoa pointed out.

"We'll just see where he's going and then come right back."

Kekoa sighed. I could tell she was less than thrilled with the idea of following him, but when I started down the path she fell in beside me. We followed quietly to avoid detection. When the man we'd been following reached the beach he joined a tall, thin woman with long black hair who was walking hand in hand with a mad dressed in black.

"It's going to be hard to tell everyone apart with them all dressed alike," Kekoa whispered.

"Yeah, it's going to be a challenge," I agreed. "Do you know who either of the men are?"

"No. They don't look familiar."

I squinted as I considered the tall, pale man with dark hair and clothing. "I suppose we'll meet everyone at dinner tonight, although if everyone is tall, pale, thin, and wearing black, it could be difficult to tell them all apart."

Kekoa frowned. "Does the fact that other than the family members everyone appears to have embraced the Goth lifestyle make you wonder why we were invited? I mean, yeah, we went to high school with Tisha, but we certainly weren't good friends and we really haven't kept up since then, other than to run into each other from time to time. We aren't family and we certainly aren't part of the Goth crowd she currently hangs with. So why the invite?"

"I've had that same thought," I admitted. "I'm wondering if our invitation wasn't a strange last-minute impulse. I didn't even know Tisha was on Oahu until I ran into her at the farmers market a few weeks ago. She introduced me to Drusilla and we got to talking. The next thing I knew, she was asking me if I would attend her wedding. When I said yes she asked if I thought you'd be interested too. I told her I thought you would if you could get the time off from work and here we are. Do you think there's more to going on than that?"

"Like what?"

"I don't know. When I ran into Tisha she seemed fidgety. She was really nice and seemed to be genuinely happy to see me, but she seemed sort of dark and depressed. And when she introduced me to Drusilla I sensed a tension you wouldn't normally find in their relationship."

Kekoa bit her lip. "I see what you mean. I noticed the same thing when we went dress shopping. Tisha was somewhat subdued at first, although she did seem to lighten up as the day progressed. I figured she was just tired and maybe a little stressed. I'm sure planning a wedding must be exhausting."

"Yeah, I guess."

I watched the man from the beach talking to the dark-haired woman. It was obvious by the way he was flailing his arms around that they were arguing. He'd grabbed the woman's arm just before Drusilla walked toward them and said something. The man let go of the woman's arm and walked away. Luckily for us, he headed down the beach and not up the path where Kekoa and I were standing. Drusilla spoke to the thin woman, who'd remained behind, and the man she'd been with for a few minutes and then the three of them turned and walked down the beach in the opposite direction.

"What do you think that was all about?" Kekoa asked.

"I'm not sure. I have a feeling this is going to be an interesting wedding in more ways than one."

"Tell me about it. This has to be the oddest wedding I've ever attended. Let's head back. The guys will be waiting."

When we got back to the pool we found Luke and Cam chatting with an older woman with silver hair that hung straight to her waist. She was sitting next to a chubby man with a bald head who immediately reminded me of Uncle Fester from *The Addams Family*.

"Lani, Kekoa, this is Dharma and her friend, Oz."

We both nodded and said we were happy to meet them.

"Are you here for the wedding?" I asked.

"I was asked to do a blessing and Dharma was asked to do a reading," Oz informed us.

"A reading?" I asked.

"Dharma is a psychic," Oz explained. "And a good one at that."

"And you're a holy man of some sort?"

"In a manner of speaking."

I wasn't sure what he meant by that, but because I'd just met them and was a guest myself I decided not to ask.

"Have you been on the island long?" I asked conversationally.

"Always," Oz replied.

It appeared as if Dharma was sizing me up. She was staring at me in a way that sent chills down my spine and so far she hadn't said a word.

"And will you officiate at the wedding?" I asked the bald man.

"Perhaps."

I wondered what was up with all the vague. Either the guy was going to officiate at the wedding or he wasn't.

"You're friends of the bride?" Oz asked.

"Kekoa and I are," I verified. "We went to high school together, although we lost touch over the years."

I jumped when Dharma took my right hand in hers and closed her eyes. I glanced at the others. Kekoa frowned as she glanced at our joined hands, Luke shrugged, and Cam grinned, as if enjoying my discomfort. I turned to Oz, who had a look of contemplation on his face but didn't say anything.

"This is the one we've been waiting for," Dharma said after maybe fifteen very uncomfortable seconds. She looked me in the eye in a way that made me want to crawl inside my skin and hide.

"Waiting for?" I screeched in a high little voice I was certain revealed my discomfort.

Oz gave Dharma a meaningful look but didn't reply. She let my hand fall to my side and took a step back but maintained eye contact with me.

"Dharma had a premonition that a guest with a specific purpose would attend the festivities," Oz explained.

"A purpose?"

"There's no need for concern. If you're the one your role will be revealed in time," Oz assured me.

Okay, these people were creeping me out. I lowered my head to break eye contact with the woman, who was still staring at me. I looked at Kekoa, who had turned to Cam, whose smile had slipped just a bit. It appeared my friends were as freaked out as I was by this conversation. Oz gave Dharma another meaningful glance that I was unable to interpret, but it definitely contributed to my uneasy feeling.

"I guess maybe I'll skip the swim and just grab a quick shower before getting dressed for dinner," I announced after deciding it was time to bail on this conversation.

"I'll come with you," Kekoa seconded.

Dharma looked at me, her eyes boring into mine. "Do not trust what you see."

I glanced at Luke. He took my hand and gave it a squeeze. If I'd had my reservations about this wacky wedding before I was full-on creeped out now.

Chapter 3

After showering and changing our clothes Kekoa and I went down to dinner. Between Dharma's cryptic comment and the overall vibe created by the strange setting, the nagging little voice in my head that tends to warn me when things aren't as they should be was chatting away a mile a minute. I wasn't sure what was up exactly, but I had the feeling something was. I decided I'd keep my thoughts to myself for the time being but pay close attention to everything that went on that evening. When I had the chance I'd write everything down for future reference. I could be way off base, but that little voice was coaching me to begin gathering clues to solve a mystery that hadn't yet presented itself. I just hoped the mystery had something to do with a missing necklace or a clandestine tryst, not a murder.

When Kekoa and I arrived in the dining room everyone else was already seated. I intended to stop off at the head of the table and say hi to Tisha, but the server, who was dressed as a vampire, escorted us directly to our place at the table. Both Kekoa and I were seated at the opposite end of the table from Ivan and Tisha, making conversation with either of our hosts close to impossible.

Once I was in my seat Ivan took a moment to welcome us and introduce everyone to one another. After he'd completed his short welcome speech, I greeted those closest to me and then sat back to observe. After a bit I took out my cell phone and took a photo of the dining table and the people gathered around it. Luke gave me an odd look, but everyone else was engaged in conversation by this time, so no one seemed to notice my odd behavior, which suited me just fine; I preferred to fly under the radar.

There were sixteen of us at dinner that night. Sitting at the head of the table were the hosts, Ivan and Tisha, or as she was known to her Goth friends, Morticia. Ivan had on a black suit with a white dress shirt. He looked to be at least ten or fifteen years older than Tisha, although he really was a handsome man with his dark wavy hair and dark brown eyes. Tisha was dressed in a long black dress, as were quite a few of the other women at the table. Perhaps the sunshine yellow dress

Kekoa had lent me wasn't the best choice for this somber affair.

The best man, Lazarus, was sitting to Ivan's right. He was also dressed in black, though he had on a deep red dress shirt with his dark suit. He was sitting next to his date, who had been introduced as Lilith. She wore a dress in the same blood-red color as Lazarus's shirt. Lilith was, I realized, the woman who had been on the beach arguing with the man from the room across the hall, who had been introduced earlier as Cole. I was pretty sure Lazarus was the man Lilith had been walking hand in hand with prior to the argument, which put Lazarus, Lilith, Cole, and Drusilla all on the beach at the time of the argument. I wasn't sure this would prove to be an important fact in the as yet identified mystery my instinct told me was on the horizon, but it was a fact I intended to record on the list of clues I planned to create when I got back to our room.

Continuing down the right side of the table, I noted that to Lilith's right sat Cory, who wore blue jeans and a white T-shirt, who was seated next to Crystal. Crystal, who was likewise dressed casually in a bright floral peasant top, sat next to Luke, who wore a plaid shirt with dark blue dress pants, and I sat to his right.

Across the table, Drusilla sat to Tisha's left. Next to her was her date, Damien. Both were dressed in black. To Damien's left sat a woman who was introduced as Raven, who we learned was Cole's guest and sat to her left. Both were dressed in black with purple accents. Based on the information currently available, I decided Raven must have been the woman we'd heard arguing with Cole in the hall. This too would be added to my list of clues.

Kekoa, wearing a pretty pink dress, sat to his left, and Cam, decked out in khakis and a light blue shirt, was seated to her left.

Buck and Bunny sat at the far end of the table, across from Ivan and Tisha. I noticed that Buck was dressed in a plaid shirt, dress jeans, and cowboy boots, while Bunny had on a shin-length dress with a flowered print.

As our first course was served, a delicious lobster bisque in a blood-red base. I studied the body language of everyone at the table. Both Ivan and Tisha were smiling and chatting, but anyone who looked closely would see their smiles didn't quite reach their eyes. They sat together but never really looked at each other, seeming to prefer to chat with those closest to them at the table. I'd never met Ivan and therefore didn't have an opinion of him as a potential husband for Tisha, but I wanted her to be happy, so I really hoped there wasn't trouble looming in paradise.

Cory, who was seated between Lilith and Crystal, looked bored. Crystal was chatting with Luke, who sat to her right, and Lilith was busy glaring at both Raven and Cole, who were seated on the opposite side of the table. I wondered if Lilith, who was breathtakingly beautiful, was the *she* Raven wanted to see gone. This too, I decided, would be added to my list of possible clues.

Drusilla was chatting with Tisha, basically ignoring Damien, who seemed happy talking with Raven. Based on the meaningful looks Damien and Raven were exchanging, I was willing to bet the two either had been lovers in the past or were working their way up to being lovers in the future. Interesting observation or important clue? At this point I had no way to know for certain, but this would go on my list as well.

Cole sat quietly eating and observing those around him. Our eyes met briefly, and I knew in an instant that he was as interested in sizing everyone up as I was.

Of all the people seated around the table, Buck and Bunny appeared to be having the best time. Both were attacking their food with gusto and seemed to have genuine smiles on their faces as they chatted with Cam and Kekoa.

The cook, who was dressed as a mummy, brought salads to the table with the vampire server, as the butler, who continued to maintain the ruse of being blind with his dark glasses and calculated manner, cleared away the soup bowls. The salad was made of fresh greens, goat cheese, beets, and candied walnuts. I wondered whether the beets were there for taste or color. It did seem that red and black with a dash of deep purple were common themes for the weekend.

"The food's delicious," Cam, who was sitting directly across from me, commented as the mummy brought out the main dish, rare prime rib with red potatoes.

"I told you the food would be out of this world," I responded.

Kekoa made a comment about the burgundy glaze that was offered as an optional sauce for the meat as Drusilla whispered something to Tisha before excusing herself and leaving the room. Damien continued to chat with Raven, apparently unconcerned that his date had left.

After dinner everyone retired to the parlor, where drinks were being served, except Damien, who I assumed was checking on Drusilla, who'd never rejoined us, and Raven, who said she had a headache. I'd noticed quite a bit of tension in the room despite the fact that Ivan was doing his best to keep the conversation light and lively.

I was on my way over to say hi to Tisha and Ivan when Ivan's brother, Buck, intercepted me. "Can I get you another drink, sugar? I'm heading that way."

"No, thank you. I'm fine for the time being. It was nice of you to offer."

"It's the Texas way to make sure all the guests are seen to."

"I heard you were from Texas. My friend Luke is too." Luke had been born and raised on a large family ranch in Texas that his father still owned. Unlike his four siblings, who'd stayed close to home after reaching adulthood, Luke had moved around a bit, living first in New York and now Hawaii.

"Yes, we chatted a bit. Seems we know a lot of the same people. Never expected to run into another Texan at this nightmare of a wedding."

"Nightmare?"

"That's what Ivan has been calling his shindig."

"That seems odd."

Buck shrugged. "Well, Ivan is an odd one. Always has been. Initially I didn't even want to come, but my brother's future bride had a chat with my Bunny and the next thing I knew, we were on a plane heading west."

"It seems like you're having a good time."

"Surprisingly, I am. Bunny said to go with the flow, and that's what I'm doing. In fact, I'm going to head over to the cute little vampire at the bar and order up another whiskey."

I scanned the parlor. "Where *is* Bunny?"

"She went up to bed shortly after Morticia did. It's been a long day."

I glanced around. Tisha wasn't in the room, although I hadn't noticed her leave. Darn, I'd really wanted to talk to her. Ivan was still in the room and was sitting at the bar, where the woman who had first been introduced as a maid was serving drinks. "Okay, well, it was nice talking to you."

"You too, sugar."

Luke joined me after Buck walked away. I had to admit he really did clean up well. "Buck tells me the two of you know some of the same people in Texas."

"We do." Luke nodded. "Texas is a big state, but the ranching community is made up of a lot of families that have been in the same areas for multiple generations, making for a pretty tight-knit group."

I looked around the room again. Buck was still chatting with the vampire bartender, although Ivan, who had been at the bar, had left the room shortly after his brother joined him there. Cory and Crystal were chatting with Kekoa and Cam, and Cole was sitting in the corner, chatting with Lilith and Lazarus. It seemed they'd mended fences after their altercation on the beach.

"I was hoping to talk to Tisha, but it looks like she's gone up to bed," I said to Luke.

"She's probably just busy with all the wedding preparations. You can get together with her tomorrow."

"Yeah, I guess." Luke had a point about Tisha being busy, but it seemed odd that she'd invite Kekoa and me to her wedding and then not bother to say a single word to either of us on the day we arrived. One would think, at the very least, that she'd want to be sure we'd settled in comfortably.

"I was thinking about going for a walk," Luke announced. "Care to join me?"

It appeared as if the party was beginning to break up. Cam and Kekoa had left the parlor a few minutes earlier and the others were beginning to say their good nights. I was surprised to see how late it was—almost midnight—and most of us had had to travel that day to get to the isolated island.

"I'd love to, but I need to head up to my room to make some notes first."

"Notes?"

I took Luke's hand. "I'll explain on the way."

Luke's facial expression changed from interested to amused to downright concerned as I explained that I had an intuition about something going on that hadn't happened yet.

"You're seriously taking notes because you feel they may help you solve a crime that hasn't even been committed?"

"Exactly."

I fully expected Luke to laugh, but he didn't. Instead, he not only offered to help me gather my thoughts but offered me a notepad to use to write them down. The notepad was in his computer case, so we headed to his room.

"Okay; where do we start?" he asked after suggesting he'd take things down as I dictated.

"The first odd thing that happened today was the argument Kekoa and I overheard coming from the room across the hall from ours. When I met them at dinner, I decided the fight was between Cole and Raven."

"And what were they arguing about?" Luke asked.

"Raven was upset that someone was here. She wanted Cole to get rid of whoever she was. Later, I saw Cole fighting with Lilith on the beach, so at this point I'm assuming Lilith is the woman Raven was upset about."

Luke jotted that down. "What else?"

"Along the same chain of thought, I noticed Cole, Lazarus, and Lilith all chatting together in the parlor. Raven had left the party, but I assumed, based on what I witnessed, that Cole and Lilith made up." I tapped my forefinger on my chin as I considered what I'd observed. "The only other thing that might be important is that Lazarus, Lilith, Cole, and Drusilla were all on the beach together at the time of the altercation, and it appeared Dru was the one who broke it up."

Luke paused with his pen in the air as I stopped speaking for a moment. "I guess that does it for now. It's hard to try to gather meaningful clues for a mystery that hadn't happened yet. Oh, wait—Damien and Raven. I'm sure there's something going on between them. Either they've been lovers at some point or they're working up to it now."

I noticed a barely discernable smile on Luke's face. I wasn't sure if he actually believed that my inner voice had the down low on what was going to occur on the island or if he was just going along with me. Either way I loved him for his effort.

"Anything else?"

"No, that's it for now. As long as we're going for a walk, how about a swim?" I suggested. "The air feels particularly heavy tonight."

"Okay. I'll pop into the bathroom and change and then we'll head to your room so you can slip into a swimsuit."

When we arrive at the room I shared with Kekoa, I was surprised to find she wasn't there. When I'd realized she and Cam had left the party I'd just assumed they'd headed off to bed. On the other hand, it was a warm evening, and a dip before bed seemed like just the thing. Maybe Cam and Kekoa had had the same idea as we had and gone for a swim.

Cam and Kekoa weren't in the pool, so we decided to head down the sandy beach trail to the ocean. It was a dark night, heavy clouds covering the moon and stars. Although it had cooled somewhat, it was still muggy.

Luke and I didn't see Cam and Kekoa on the beach, so we dove into the warm sea. We swam and played and kissed under the stars until our energy was spent. Then we returned to the beach, where we wrapped ourselves in the towels we'd brought with us.

"Wind's starting to pick up a bit," Luke observed as I felt the warm air caress my skin.

"Yeah. I noticed the clouds on the horizon when I was out with Kekoa. I thought the storm would be here by now, but it appears to have been delayed." I lifted my face to the dark horizon. "I think we're still in for quite a storm, even if it is late. I suppose we should head back before it arrives."

"I agree we're in for a doozy, but I checked the weather report earlier and I think we have a few hours at least before the worst of it hits landfall." Luke pulled me into his arms and held me tight against his chest as the waves crashed onto the shore. There were times such as this that I wanted to give myself to Luke completely; if only I could overcome my fear of a broken heart.

"I thought we'd run into Cam and Kekoa down here," I said as I rested my head on his chest and melted into his warmth. I could hear his heart beating beneath my ear, which was both comforting and sensual.

Luke caressed my back as we stood chest to chest. "Maybe they were on the beach but already had headed back in before we arrived."

"You'd think we would have passed them." I tightened my arms around Luke's waist.

"I'm not all that familiar with this island, but it seems reasonable that there might be more than one path leading to and from the water."

"I guess that makes sense."

Luke lifted my head so we were looking into each other's eyes. He leaned forward and kissed me oh so softly. I felt every nerve ending in my body begin to tingle as he slid his hands down my arms and then to encircled my waist. The towel I had wrapped around my body fell onto the sand and dropped to my feet. Luke let his towel slide down his body as well before pulling me into his arms and kissing me, first gently and then more deeply as the longings we'd both denied ourselves demanded to be heard. I'd become completely lost in Luke's kiss to the point where I was no longer aware of my surroundings when he groaned and took a step back.

I was momentarily disoriented but quickly realized we were practically making love in public. Luke reached down and picked up our towels, then wrapped one around his waist and the other around my shoulders. He leaned forward and kissed me on the top of the head in a very brotherly fashion. I had to admit my thoughts about Luke at that moment weren't brotherly at all.

He laced his fingers through mine as we started back up the path to the pool and patio. There was an outdoor shower where we could rinse off the sand and sea before continuing on inside. Luke helped me rinse my long black hair as I stood under the warm spray. It was an extremely erotic sensation to have his fingers caressing my head as he washed the salt away. I found myself wishing Kekoa and I weren't sharing a room. Of course Luke had his own room, but although I was tempted, I still wasn't sure I wanted to take that next step in our relationship quite yet. I cared for Luke. In fact, it wouldn't be a stretch to say I might even love him. And I definitely was attracted to him, probably more so than to any other man I'd ever met. But Luke was a displaced cowboy temporarily living the Hawaiian dream and I knew in my heart that if I were to give myself to him completely I'd never be able to stand back and wish him well when he walked out of my life forever.

When we got to my room I found Kekoa still wasn't there. "Should we look for them?" I asked.

"Do you think they might be together in Cam's room?"

I squinched up my nose as I considered Luke's question. "I don't think so. Cam and Kekoa are just friends."

Luke smiled. "Like you are I are just friends?"

"No. Like Cam and I are just friends. I doubt they're together in the way you're suggesting. Maybe they're in Cam's room just hanging out. I guess we should check to be sure."

Cam's room was empty as well.

"Maybe we should look for them," I said. "Let's change out of our wet things and then head back downstairs. Maybe they went back to the party for another drink."

Luke shrugged. "Seems unlikely, but if it will make you feel better we'll look. Give me a few minutes to shower and dress. I'll meet you back here when I'm ready."

He and I showered and put on fresh clothes, then headed back down to the parlor. A quick look around showed us that Cory and Buck were the only two still in the room. They were sitting at the bar, pounding down drinks.

"Have you seen Cam and Kekoa?" I asked them.

"No," Cory answered. "Not since before you left."

"And the others?"

"They all began to head up not long after you did," Buck offered. "Do the two of you want to join us for a drink?"

"No, thank you," I answered. "We'll see you both tomorrow."

Luke and I left the parlor and paused in the hallway.

"Now what?" Luke asked.

"I don't know. Let's check the rest of the common areas and then head back out to the pool if we haven't found them.

We're on an island; they couldn't have wandered off too far."

Luke and I looked in the kitchen, dining room, living room, media room, gym, atrium, and library. The door to Ivan's office was locked and we didn't think it prudent to start knocking on bedroom doors, so we checked our rooms and Cam's one more time before trading our flip-flops for tennis shoes and heading back outside. The castle was huge, and while there were hallways we'd yet to explore, I couldn't imagine Cam and Kekoa would explore them without permission from our host, so I doubted we'd find them in a different wing.

We checked the pool and the patio, which were still deserted, as well as the pool house and the groundskeeper's shed. The wind had picked up somewhat, causing a louder rustling than had been present before.

"What if something happened to them?" I was beginning to get scared. I'd had a premonition about a mystery, but I'd never imagined it would involve missing friends.

"Like what?"

"I don't know. Maybe they went for a walk and got too close to the edge of the cliff and fell, or maybe they decided to check out the waterfall and got lost in the jungle. Maybe someone kidnapped them or murdered them." I was becoming hysterical. "There are any number of things that could have occurred." A single tear slid down my cheek.

Luke pulled me into his arms and hugged me hard. "I know you've been having premonitions that something would happen ever since your weird encounter with Dharma this afternoon, but I'm sure they're fine. Let's go back to the house and find some flashlights. We'll look around the castle one more time and if we don't find them we'll come back out here and look around the grounds more thoroughly."

I wiped the tear from my cheek and looked up at the sky. It was inky black, with no light from the moon showing through. I figured we had maybe thirty minutes before the rain hit and if Cam and Kekoa were in trouble I intended to find them. "Okay, but let's hurry. I don't think we have a lot of time."

When we returned to the castle we ran into the vampire maid/server/bartender who set us up with flashlights. She told us she hadn't seen our friends and had just done a sweep of the place to make sure things were in order before she retired for the night. Even Buck and Cory had gone upstairs, so the common areas on the lower floor were deserted with the exception of the vampire maid, Luke, and me. By the time Luke and I made it down to the beach it was starting to sprinkle.

Although I hadn't had a chance to explore the entire island yet, I'd observed that there was a deep channel leading up to a protected bay where the boat dock was located. There was a road leading from the dock to the castle, which sat at the center of the island several hundred feet above sea level. From the castle there was a trail leading down to a wide, sandy beach, which was where Luke and I currently stood. It looked as if you could only walk along the beach maybe a half mile in any direction before you hit the cliffs, which ran along the back side of the island. The area surrounding the castle and the groomed grounds that bordered it was made up of dense jungle. Other than the path Mr. Graves had pointed out that led to the waterfall, I hadn't noticed any other groomed trails, but I hadn't had all that much time to look around yet.

As the wind increased in velocity, the waves grew in size, crashing onto the beach with loud bangs. Luke and I walked the beach, calling out Kekoa and Cam's names, but I doubted our voices could be heard over the sound of the waves. Hiking into the interior of the jungle on a dark, stormy night wasn't a good idea, so after we covered the beach we decided to head back to the house to alert the others that our friends were missing. As we started up the beach path toward the house, I heard a loud pop in the distance.

"That sounded like a gunshot," I said.

Chapter 4

"Yeah." Luke looked around at our surroundings. "I think it came from that direction." He pointed into the dense jungle that bordered the groomed area closer to the house.

"Should we check it out or should we go back to the house to tell someone?" I looked toward where we'd heard the shot and then back toward the castle, which looked to be completely dark. It seemed everyone had gone to bed.

"I don't know. Let's head back up to the house and look around. The sound might not have come from the jungle. Some of the people inside must have heard it."

"Do you think the shot came from inside the castle?"

Luke frowned. "I hope not."

We made our way up the sandy trail from the beach to the pool deck. The wind and rain made the trail more difficult to climb and we were both out of breath by the time we reached the top. There was a light coming from the edge of the jungle.

It looked as if there was someone else out and about with a flashlight. The shot must have woken someone, though it was equally possible the light was coming from a flashlight carried by the shooter. At this point we had no idea why someone would be shooting off a gun in the middle of the night, but we felt it best not to risk confronting whoever the person was directly.

Luke and I decided to follow from a distance. We couldn't make out much about the person carrying the flashlight, other than that they were dressed in black, which told us very little given the company we were in.

We followed the dark figure back to the castle. After going in through the back door the person carrying the flashlight took off a black hooded cape.

"Drusilla?" I asked as the person's identity was revealed.

"Lani, what were you doing out in the rain?"

"We were looking for Cam and Kekoa. Have you seen them?"

"No. I came down for something to eat and heard what sounded like a gunshot, so I went to investigate, but I didn't find anything. I guess it was just my imagination. The wind is making all sorts of clatter."

"I'm worried about Cam and Kekoa. It's not like them to just take off, but we've checked everywhere, including the pool house and the groundskeeper's shed, and they seem to have just disappeared. Do you know of any other structures we can check? Maybe someplace not attached to the house or grounds where they might have taken shelter?"

"You've been through the entire castle?"

"We checked everything we had access to in this wing. Do you think they could have wandered into a different area of the building?"

"Ivan keeps the doors to the hallways locked when he has guests. This is a large property and he doesn't want anyone to wander off and get lost. The only areas your friends would have access to are this first floor, which includes the living room, parlor, kitchen, dining room, media room, library, gym, and atrium, as well as the bedrooms on the second and third floor. Ivan has an office on this floor, but he normally keeps it locked as well."

"We've looked all those places except the bedrooms. We hate to wake everyone up if we don't have to."

"I guess you can check the cemetery."

"The cemetery?" Luke asked.

"There's a large mausoleum less than a quarter of a mile from here. A footpath leads to an enclosed structure at the north edge of the garden. I suppose if they were out walking and the storm hit they might have taken shelter inside."

I doubted Cam and Kekoa would wander that far away and didn't like the idea of checking out a mausoleum in the middle of a storm on a dark, windy night, but unless Cam and Kekoa had slipped into their rooms while Luke and I were searching for them, that was exactly what I was going to do. A quick check of the house including their rooms proved futile, so I had Dru draw us a map and Luke and I headed back out. If they weren't waiting out the storm in the mausoleum I was waking everyone up and organizing a search party.

The cemetery was located, as Dru had indicated, less than a quarter of a mile beyond the far edge of the garden. As Dru had said, there was a dirt path that wove through the dense foliage until it eventually led to a clearing that was dotted with tombstones. The mausoleum was located at the rear of the clearing, a large stone structure with a wooden door that was now cracked open. Luke pried the door open enough so that we could look inside.

"Kekoa," I called as I slipped inside the narrow opening with my flashlight in front of me.

I heard a groan.

"Are you in here?" I called again.

Luke slipped in behind me. On the surface it didn't look like the open space contained anything but coffins, cobwebs, and spiders. I shuddered as I wiped a cobweb from my cheek so I could get a better view of the rows and rows of coffins. I'd heard people describe the sensation of a chill running up their spine, but until I heard a thunking sound coming from one of the coffins I really had never experienced it.

"Did you hear that?" I whispered to Luke.

"Yes."

"Do you think there's a vampire in that coffin?"

"Despite the fact we're spending the weekend in Dracula's castle, I think that's highly unlikely."

I heard the thunking again. "What should we do?"

"I think we should open it."

"Are you kidding me? We're in a mausoleum on a private island in a storm in the middle of the night and you want to open a coffin that has a noise coming from inside?"

"It could be Cam or Kekoa. We have to."

"Yeah, okay," I agreed. I tried to avoid the cobwebs and prayed that the something running up my arm wasn't a spider as I looked around for something to use as a stake. I'm not an expert on vampires, but in the movies the vampire slayer always uses a wooden stake to kill the vampire for good. There wasn't anything handy, so I simply held my breath as Luke slowly opened the lid.

"Cam!" I yelled when I realized it was him lying inside the coffin with his hands and feet tied and a large piece of duct tape over his mouth. "Are you okay?" I asked after Luke pulled away the tape and lifted Cam out of the coffin so he could untie him.

"Kekoa...is she with you?" Cam asked.

"No. We came to look for both of you. What happened?" I asked.

"Kekoa wanted to go for a walk and I volunteered to go with her. We headed to the beach, where we could see two people involved in an intimate embrace. We didn't want to disturb them, so we turned around to come back up the path when all of a sudden everything went dark. I came to in the coffin just a minute or two before I heard you calling. I've never been so scared in my life. I thought for sure I'd been buried alive."

"Maybe Kekoa is in one of the other coffins," Luke suggested.

I looked around the room. There were at least a couple dozen coffins. "Yeah, but which one?"

"Kekoa," Luke called as loud as he could.

The response was complete silence.

"God, I hope she isn't…" Cam left the sentence unfinished.

I turned to the coffin closest to me and opened the lid. It was empty. Luke and Cam both helped me to open coffins, all of which were empty.

"Oh, God," I murmured when I'd opened the fifth or sixth one.

"Kekoa?" Cam paled.

"No."

Luke walked across the mausoleum and joined me. In the coffin in a long white dress was Dharma. She looked like a bride lying on her back with her eyes closed and her arms crossed over her chest. Her skin was as white as her dress and a trail of blood started at her chest, ran down one side, and pooled around her.

"It looks like she's been shot," Luke commented.

I glanced at Cam, whose look of concern had turned to terror.

"Kekoa," Cam yelled.

The three of us began frantically opening coffins until we finally found Kekoa. She was still unconscious but breathing. Luke picked her up and we started back to the house, praying the entire way that she wouldn't die. She was as pale as a sheet and had a bloody gash on her head that made me want to fall to my knees and cry.

"I'll take her into the parlor and put her down on the sofa. You go get help," Luke instructed me.

My first instinct was to alert our host as to what had occurred, but the door leading from the third floor to others above was locked. I'd noticed which room Buck and Bunny had been assigned to when we arrived, and because they seemed the most normal of the group of visitors, I decided to bang on their door.

"What is it?" a groggy-looking Buck, dressed only in boxer shorts, answered the door.

"It's Cam and Kekoa. Someone hit them over the head. Kekoa is still unconscious. Can you help us?"

"I'll see what I can do. Let me grab some pants."

"Hurry. We're in the parlor."

A few seconds after I arrived downstairs Buck, followed by Bunny in a terry-cloth robe, joined us.

"I can't imagine who could have done this," Bunny said as Buck, who'd had some medical training in the army, examined the gash on Kekoa's head.

"She's going to need a stitch or two, but the gash is actually pretty small," Buck announced.

I thought I might pass out, but I held it together while Buck opened a medical kit he apparently traveled with. Buck explained that both his training during the four years he'd served in the military, as well as his life as a cowboy, had taught him it was best to always be prepared for whatever might occur.

Buck looked at Bunny. "I know this makes you squeamish. Why don't you go on back to the room? I'll be there in a bit."

"Maybe that would be best." Bunny turned and walked back to the staircase.

Poor Bunny. She looked paler than Kekoa.

"Is she going to be okay?" I asked after Bunny left.

"Her respiration and heartbeat seem steady and it looks as if she's starting to come to. We'll need to watch for symptoms that would indicate a concussion, but my guess is that she'll be fine."

"Do you remember anything at all about what happened?" Buck asked Cam as he continued to work on Kekoa.

"Not really. Like I told Luke and Lani, Kekoa and I were walking on the beach and we saw two people, both dressed in black, in an intimate embrace. We didn't want to interrupt them, so we turned around to go back up the path just as someone must have hit us from behind. I don't remember anything after that until I woke up in the coffin."

Kekoa's eyelids began to flutter and she began to wake up just about the time Buck finished stitching her up.

"What happened?" she asked.

I briefly explained that she'd been knocked out. "Do you know who hit you?"

"No. I don't remember anything. Cam and I were taking a walk. Oh, God, Cam. Is he okay?"

"Right here." Cam stepped forward and wrapped Kekoa's hand in his.

"Thank God. What happened? Did you see anything?"

"Not after we turned around to come back to the castle," Cam told her.

Kekoa put her free hand to her head. I wasn't a doctor, but I wondered if it would be okay to give her some painkillers. Buck asked her to sit up, which made her dizzy and nauseous, so he had her lie back down. He wanted to wait until she was able to sit up on her own before we gave her anything for the pain.

"We should get Kekoa to the hospital," I insisted.

"The boat shuttle left after dropping us off," Luke pointed out.

"I think we need to wake Ivan to see if there's a way to get to the mainland," Buck said. "I can't believe he'd live on this island without a means of transportation."

"The door to the upper floor is locked," I explained.

Buck frowned. "Seems like a needless thing to do, given that the castle is occupied by family and friends."

"I agree. This whole weekend is beyond weird."

"Did anyone happen to notice which rooms the staff occupy?" Luke asked.

No one was aware of which rooms belonged to them. We speculated that the staff might be housed in a separate wing of the castle.

"Does anyone else feel like they went to sleep and woke up in a horror movie?" Cam asked.

No one answered, but it seemed apparent we all shared Cam's sentiment.

"I'm having a hard time dealing with the fact that anyone we met this evening could be responsible for this," Buck said.

"Tisha told me that you and Ivan didn't grow up together. How well do you really know your brother?" I asked Buck.

"Not well at all. In fact, I hadn't seen him in over twenty years until today. I'm still not sure we should have come. Somehow Ivan's intended found out about me and Bunny and called our house. Bunny spoke to her, and by the end of the conversation both women were convinced it was important for us to be here. To be honest, I didn't want to come, but Bunny has a way of getting what she wants, and what she wanted was to meet my brother."

"So Bunny had never met Ivan?"

"No. The last time I saw him was just before I joined the army. I met Bunny after I left it."

"Maybe we can find the maid or someone who has a key to the upper floors," I murmured, getting back to the matter at hand.

"I'm okay," Kekoa assured me. "Just a little dizzy. I don't need to go to the hospital, so we don't need to wake anyone."

"Are you sure? You were unconscious for a long time."

"I'm fine, really. The nausea is gone and the dizziness is passing."

"Do you think we should call the police?" I wondered. "I certainly would feel better if one, or even all, of my five cop brothers were here."

"That was my thought exactly when we found Dharma, but I'm sure with the storm the satellite signal is out," Luke informed me.

"Dharma?" Buck asked. "Who's Dharma?"

Luke explained about the man and woman we'd met at the pool earlier in the day, and that we'd found Dharma shot to death, her body left in one of the coffins in the mausoleum.

"Well, this changes things quite a bit. Maybe we should try to wake Ivan," Buck decided. "There must be someone with a key."

"We don't know who did it," Luke reminded us. "It might be best not to alert the killer that we found the body in the mausoleum until we have a plan to deal with them. There isn't anything we can do for Dharma at this point and it's only a few hours until daybreak. Let's all try to get some sleep and maybe in the morning the storm will have passed and the satellites will be back online. If not, we can ask Ivan about an alternate source of transportation and/or communication."

"Someone should keep an eye on Kekoa and Cam," Buck pointed out.

"Lani and I will wait up with them until we're sure they're okay. Why don't you go ahead and turn in? Who knows what tomorrow might bring?"

"It has been a long day for Bunny and me," Buck admitted. "We flew into Honolulu from Dallas just an hour before we met you all at the boat dock."

"Lock your bedroom door," I cautioned.

"Will do." Buck got up and gathered his supplies. "See you all in the morning," he added as he headed for the stairs.

Luke and I settled Kekoa and Cam in the two queen beds in the room I shared with my cousin. Luke moved a couple of comfortable chairs together for the two of us to sit in while we watched over them.

"How are you feeling?" I asked both of them as I snuggled into my chair.

"Better," Kekoa answered. "I still have a headache, but the nausea and dizziness is completely gone."

"This whole thing is so incredibly unbelievable," Cam said. "Who would knock us out and put us in coffins?"

"Yeah, and while Dharma had an unsettling presence, who would kill her?" I added.

"Do you think whoever did this meant to kill us?" Kekoa asked.

"I don't think so," Luke answered. "The lids to the coffins in the mausoleum weren't in any way locked or secured. The only reason Cam couldn't easily get out of the one he was in was because his hands and feet were tied. Chances are he eventually would have realized he could push open the lid by sitting up and lifting it with his hands, which were tied in front of him."

"I can't believe that hadn't occurred to me."

"When we arrived at the mausoleum you had just regained consciousness and were still in a state of panic. If you had been given a chance to calm down you would have figured it out," Luke assured him.

"If the motive wasn't to kill us why put us inside them in the first place?" Cam asked.

Luke frowned. "I don't know. All the coffins we opened with the exception of the three that held you, Kekoa, and Dharma were empty. Ever since we found you guys I've been asking myself why there would be so many empty coffins."

"Zombies?" I guessed.

Luke laughed. "No, not zombies. I was thinking more along the lines of the coffins being used for some sort of a ritual or a role-playing game."

I frowned. "A ritual?"

"We're on a private island in a very expensive mansion that was built to replicate Dracula's castle. I'm going to go out on a limb and say that Ivan's fascination with Dracula runs deeper than mere fascination. It sort of makes sense that there would be coffins on the property for use in role-playing games."

I couldn't help but wonder what Tisha had gotten herself in to. The idea that a group of adults would voluntarily close themselves into coffins was beyond the borders of my imagination.

"Okay, so assuming the person who put Cam and Kekoa in the coffins didn't do so with the intention of killing them, what possible reason could they have for doing so?"

"I keep coming back to the idea that they were simply at the wrong place at the wrong time and the coffins were a convenient place to temporarily stash them," Luke answered.

"It did sort of seem that way," Cam agreed. "Whoever hit us came out of nowhere. They might have followed us down to the beach, but it seemed more as if they were already there when we stumbled onto the couple."

"Maybe the couple wasn't actually a couple, if you know what I mean," Kekoa joined in.

"So the two individuals on the beach might have been cheating on their partners and didn't want to be found out," I theorized. "I guess I can understand that, but it didn't sound like the person who hit you was one of the two who were making out. Doesn't it seem odd that someone might have been watching this couple in the first place?"

"Maybe the person was watching the couple and didn't want them interrupted, or maybe the person who hit us didn't want to have their presence revealed," Cam suggested.

"What about the fact that we saw Drusilla returning to the house from the direction we now know was of the mausoleum?" I pointed out. "Do you think she could be responsible for all this?"

"If she is, she had help. There's no way she could have carried Cam from the beach to the mausoleum on her own," Luke pointed out.

"That's true. Still, Dru did leave the party before we even finished dinner. I have a gut feeling she's involved in some way."

Kekoa yawned. "I'm so tired."

"You should stay awake a little longer," I said encouragingly. "Just to be sure you're all right."

"One thing is for certain: if the storm lets up I'm going home," Kekoa said. "Being hit over the head and closed up in a coffin isn't what I signed on for."

"I'm right there with you," Cam agreed.

I wanted to join the going-home bandwagon, but I couldn't help but feel responsible for figuring out what had happened to Dharma. She'd seemed to indicate that she was waiting for me and now she was dead. I wondered now if she knew she would die and was counting on me to figure out who had killed her.

Chapter 5

Saturday, October 29

Luke and I stayed with Kekoa and Cam for most of the night. At some point Buck knocked on the door and told us it was probably fine to leave them and get some sleep ourselves. Cam was sleeping in my bed and it made sense for me to sleep in his, but I was feeling unsettled after everything that had happened so I ended up sharing a bed with Luke. It was all very frustratingly platonic, which was probably wise given my emotional state, but it did occur to me that it might be time to take a second look at my decision to keep Luke firmly in the casual dating zone. Yes, I had a good reason to keep him at arm's length, but I was beginning to have a stronger reason to let him in.

I thought I'd feel weird with Luke next to me and have a hard time falling asleep despite the fact that we were both fully clothed, but as it turned out having him close made me feel safe and I fell asleep almost before my head hit the pillow. When I awoke he was gone from the room, but there was a note letting me know I should meet him downstairs.

I glanced out the window, which had been adorned with blackout curtains like the rest of the castle but I had opened. The storm had gotten worse while we slept and the sky was so dark that it could still have been nighttime. I snuggled down under the heavy comforter for another moment while I let myself come fully awake.

After watching the rain slam into the window for a few minutes I rolled out of bed and headed into the bathroom. I showered and dressed in the same clothes I'd changed into the previous evening. I combed out my long hair and fashioned it into a braid, then headed down the stairs to join the others. I found Luke in the kitchen chatting with the cook, who was wearing regular clothes today rather than her mummy costume.

"Morning," I said as I poured myself a cup of coffee from the pot.

"You're up earlier than I thought you'd be," Luke commented as the cook left the room.

"The wind was slamming into the window, which was making it rattle, but I didn't want to sleep too late anyway. Where is everyone?"

Luke filled me in. "Cam and Kekoa are eating breakfast in bed. Both feel better and plan to get up and join the living once they have a chance to clean up a bit. Ivan and Tisha and Buck and Bunny aren't down yet. Raven came down and grabbed some coffee, then went back upstairs. I haven't seen Cole. Lazarus, Lilith, Drusilla, and Damien are in the dining room, which is where I was heading."

"How about Cory and Crystal?"

"I haven't seen them."

"Are Cam and Kekoa still talking about leaving?" I wondered.

"I think they'd like to, but the storm really hasn't let up so there's no way a boat or even a helicopter can access the island. I guess we're all stuck here for the time being. Are you hungry?"

"Starving."

"The cook—whose name is Mrs. Baker, by the way—has a buffet laid out in the dining room. Grab your coffee and we'll join the others."

Lazarus, Lilith, Dru, and Damien hadn't been downstairs when Luke and I had found Cam, Kekoa, and Dharma, so none of them had heard about what had happened. I watched the faces of all four for some reaction that would hint that one or more of them had been the lowlife bloodsuckers who had injured my friends and killed a psychic, but they all looked genuinely surprised. I did notice Lilith exchange a meaningful look with Damien, but there seemed to be a lot going on behind the scenes, so I wasn't sure if the glance had to do with the story Luke was telling or something else entirely.

Lilith, Lazarus, Damien, and Dru seemed to be part of Ivan's inner circle, and I suspected they might have spent more time on the island than any of the others. I wanted to ask about the coffins in the mausoleum, but I wasn't sure how well my inquiry would be received if the group did, as Luke suspected, use the coffins for some sort of ritual or role-play. Instead, I asked about the cemetery in general.

"The cemetery as well as the mausoleum were on the island before Ivan bought the property," Damien explained.

"So someone lived on the island before the castle was built?" I clarified.

"A bunch of someones," Damien answered. "The island was originally a coffee plantation. There was a small town where the castle now stands that was wiped out in a hurricane more than two decades ago. Ivan leveled what remained after he bought the island and built the castle."

"I didn't realize the island was that big," Luke commented.

"When you arrived you came from the north, which is the flattest part of the island. When you have a chance to explore you'll see it's a lot bigger than you probably imagined."

"And the coffee bushes?" I asked.

"Many died over the years and were swallowed up by the jungle, but there are still quite a few toward the center of the island that have survived."

"Once the storm lets up you should take the trail Mr. Graves pointed out yesterday that winds its way up the mountain and leads to the waterfall as well as the interior of the island," Drusilla suggested. "You'll be able to see remnants of some of the other buildings that were partially destroyed but Ivan hasn't leveled yet."

"So the entire island was inhabited in the past?" Luke asked.

"A good part of it. As I said, the town was located where the castle now sits, but there are quite a few deserted homes dotted here and there throughout the jungle."

"And the mausoleum?" I asked. "Do you happen to know who's buried there?"

"No one." Damien laughed. He looked a lot less like a demon and a lot more like a very handsome man dressed for Halloween when he smiled.

"You really shouldn't be giving away all of Ivan's secrets," Lilith scolded.

Damien winked at Lilith. "I think we both know I haven't given away all our undead prince's secrets."

"I think we should change the subject before someone says something that's going to land us all in hot water," Lazarus suggested. "As perfectly awesome as the dreary weather is, I find it's put a damper on my plans for the day."

"You and Lilith can join Drusilla and me in the dungeon," Damien offered.

Lazarus looked at Lilith, who shrugged. "Sure. I have no idea where Cole has gone off to and we both know Raven won't make an appearance until sunset."

Shortly after that, the four made their excuses and headed toward the hallway at the back of the property, which I hadn't yet had the opportunity to explore. I wondered if they, as Ivan's close friends, had access to the entire castle.

"Okay, that was weird," I said after they were gone.

"I have to agree."

I nibbled on the end of a strip of bacon as I tried to make sense of everything. There seemed to be a lot going on that appeared to be connected, but I wondered if it really was. I remembered Dharma warning me not to trust what I saw and sat back to look at Luke, who had continued to eat but clearly had a lot on his mind. "Kekoa and I were wondering yesterday exactly why Tisha had invited us to the wedding in the first place. It's not like we're superclose, and we certainly don't fit in with Tisha and Ivan's other friends. But after what happened last night, I'm thinking everything might have somehow been staged."

"Staged? A woman is dead. Who would stage a death?"

"I don't know. What I do know, though, is that Dharma said some odd things when we first met. Then, when we found her body, she was wearing what looked like a wedding gown, and the strangest thing of all is that a woman is dead and everyone is just going about their business as if nothing has happened. Shouldn't people be outraged or frightened or both?"

"I see your point." Luke frowned.

He sipped his coffee and I turned my attention to my eggs. The weekend was turning out to be the oddest I'd ever experienced.

Crystal, dressed in casual shorts and a tank top, walked into the dining room. She had a thoughtful look on her face as she dished up a small plate of food and sat down across from Luke and me. "I ran into Bunny in the hall. She told me what happened."

"I'd wondered if you'd heard," I responded.

"Do Ivan and Tisha know?"

"I'm not sure," I said. "When we checked last night the door that leads to the upper floors was locked, so we weren't able to inform them, and they haven't been down yet this morning. We did tell Drusilla, Damien, Lazarus, and Lilith, however, so I suppose they might have passed the news along by now."

Crystal stabbed at her eggs but never actually took a bite. I could see she was disturbed by the turn of events, which was at the very least a more normal response than that of Ivan's Goth friends'.

"I need to talk to you. Both of you. Alone," Crystal suddenly whispered in a voice so low I could barely make out what she was saying even though she was sitting directly across from me.

"Okay," I said in a slightly louder whisper. "We're alone now."

Crystal looked around. "No. Not here. Not in the castle."

I could hear the rain outside the curtain-covered window behind my chair. "It's still pouring."

Crystal bit her lip. She continued in a low voice, "When I was out walking yesterday I noticed an old cabin in the forest. It's pretty dilapidated, but it has a roof. Sort of. Anyway, I think we can talk in there without getting wet and without being overheard. It's not far if you're willing to meet us there."

"Us?" I asked.

"Me and Cory. Say in an hour? I can draw you a map and drop it off at your room."

I glanced at Luke. He shrugged.

"Okay," I said.

"I'll slide the map under your door. I don't want anyone to know we're meeting."

I nodded.

"Be careful what you say within these walls. I think someone may be listening." With that, Crystal got up and walked out.

Listening to us? Was the entire castle bugged? I thought back to the conversations I'd had the previous day. I certainly hoped it wasn't. Luke seemed to be processing everything that had just occurred. This wedding was getting stranger and stranger.

"Should we go up?" Luke asked.

"Yeah, let's check on Kekoa and Cam." I looked at my watch. "When Crystal said she'd slide the map under the bedroom door she must have meant my room with Kekoa. We'll wait there."

As soon as we entered the room, we motioned for Cam and Kekoa to remain silent. Then we turned on the radio Kekoa had brought to use as an alarm clock. I motioned that we should gather together on the same bed so we could speak without raising our voices. Once we were fairly certain we wouldn't be overheard we filled them in on the latest news.

"This is absolutely insane," Kekoa whispered. "We need to get out of here."

I glanced out the window, which was framed by the drape I'd opened the previous day. "I don't think any of us are going anywhere until the storm lets up. In the meantime I think we need to make sure we stick together."

"So Cam and I should come with you?" Kekoa asked.

"No. It'll be harder to slip away if we all leave the room. Besides, you're still weak.

Cam can stay with you while Luke and I meet Crystal and Cory. You should be fine until we get back."

"I'm more worried about you not being fine than I am about us," Kekoa corrected her. "What if Crystal and Cory are the ones who killed Dharma and attacked me and Cam, and you're walking right into their trap?"

I had to admit that if Crystal *was* the killer her plan to isolate us was perfect, but my gut told me she wasn't the lowlife who'd attacked Kekoa and Cam. "How long after you left the party was it that you were hit?"

Cam thought about it. "I guess maybe fifteen to twenty minutes."

"Luke and I left shortly after you, but we came upstairs first, so you were probably being knocked out and placed in the caskets while we were up here. At the time we left the castle Buck, the vampire bartender, Cory, Crystal, Lilith, Lazarus, and Cole were still downstairs. Drusilla had left the dining room while we were still eating, and Damien left us after dinner but before we all met in the parlor, and Raven left shortly after Damien. Tisha left us shortly after we'd gathered for drinks, followed by Bunny. Buck went to have a drink with Ivan, who left him shortly after that."

"How do you remember all that?" Cam asked. "I have a handle on who Crystal, Cory, Buck, Bunny, Tisha, and Ivan are, and Drusilla is the only one with blond hair, but the others are all just a blur."

"They all do tend to dress the same and it can get confusing, but I thought it might be important so I took notes," I answered.

"Cole is the man who was sitting next to me at dinner last night," Kekoa reminded Cam.

"Oh, yeah, the man who sat there staring at everyone but not really participating."

"Exactly, and Raven is his date, who was flirting with Drusilla's date, Damien."

"Okay, I think I'm starting to get this. Lazarus was the one sitting next to Ivan and Lilith was his very beautiful date," Cam summarized.

"Yes."

"So Cory, Crystal, Lilith, Lazarus, Buck, and Cole couldn't have hit us over the head and put us in the coffins because they were still at the party when we were put in the coffins," Cam concluded.

"Probably not," I agreed. "Although everyone other than Buck and Cory could have shot Dharma. They were the only two left in the bar when Luke and I went back to look for you. Based on the time we heard the gunshot, you were already in the coffin when Dharma was killed and placed in the mausoleum with you."

"The same person must be guilty of both hitting Cam and me and shooting Dharma because we were all disposed of in the same way," Kekoa pointed out.

"It seems likely," I answered.

I looked up to see the map being slid under the door and Luke got up to retrieve it. It looked as if the structure Crystal referred to was in the forest behind the castle. It would be convenient if we knew of a back door, but the hallways to the wings at the rear of the castle were locked, so we'd need to go out the front and skirt around the edge of the building until we found the path she'd marked.

After making sure Kekoa and Cam had everything they needed, Luke and I instructed them to lock the door behind us before we snuck down the stairs and out the front door.

The wind was blowing from the west, so we decided to make the trek around the castle on the east side. The tall stone structure partially shielded us from the wind and rain, making the journey a bit easier. The castle was so large, it actually took us quite a while to make it around to the southern side of the structure. The wind was quite a bit steadier when we turned the corner from the east side of the building to the south, so I grabbed Luke's arm to avoid getting blown away as we searched for the path Crystal had indicated we should take to find the cabin.

"I hope the trail didn't get washed away."

Both Luke and I were soaking wet by this point, but it was a warm rain, so it didn't really matter. I knew we'd dry off quickly enough once we got inside.

Luke stopped walking and looked into the distance. He placed his hand over his eyes to protect them from the driving rain. "I think we need to go that way." He pointed into the distance.

"Lead the way." I clutched his hand tighter.

The short trek from the castle to the cabin was perilous at best. While the castle had provided shelter, the path Crystal had instructed us to take was out in the open. I ducked as a coconut flew past my head. For the first time since we'd begun our journey I wondered again if Kekoa was right. If Crystal was the one who had killed Dharma and wanted Luke and me dead, sending us out into the storm was a surefire way to accomplish just that.

"I see something," Luke said. "It's just up ahead."

Thank God. There were more projectiles flying through the air than I could keep track of. It was only a matter of time before either Luke or I—or both—were hit.

Thankfully, when we arrived at the cabin we found Crystal and Cory sitting on a bench that had been built against a wall in one of the rooms, sheltered from the storm. A quick look at the dilapidated cabin had me concerned that this might not be the best place to be in a storm, but the building was old enough to have survived worse ones in the past.

"Thank you for coming." Crystal looked genuinely grateful. She and Cory were as wet as we were, so I thought whatever she had to talk to us about must be important enough to brave the storm.

Luke got right down to business. "What do you need to tell us that you couldn't say in the castle?"

"You'd better have a seat. This is kind of a long story."

Luke and I sat down on the bench that had been built into the opposite wall and waited for Crystal to continue.

"When my sister called me a while back and told me that she had left the convent I was glad. I knew she was just off on another of her tangents, that she was never actually going to complete the requirements to be a nun, so why waste everyone's time? Besides that, I had a feeling the convent she'd hooked up with wasn't a real one, at least not in the traditional sense. I don't claim to have any firsthand knowledge of how the whole thing works, but it seems to me that to be a nun you first have to be Catholic, which Tisha isn't."

I wanted to ask her about the fake convent, but I had a feeling that wasn't the point of this particular conversation, so I didn't say anything.

"As we spoke," Crystal continued, "Tisha informed me she'd left the convent because she'd met a man and was, in fact, engaged. Becoming engaged to someone she'd just met was a very Tisha thing to do, but still, I was concerned, so I pretended to be happy for her and asked to meet him."

Crystal took a deep breath. I could see the stress on her face. Again, I remained silent, waiting for her to continue.

"Several weeks went by and she never called me to set up a meeting, so I began to call her. I tried for weeks to get through to her, but all my calls went directly to voice mail. I didn't know who her fiancé was other than that his name was Ivan; I didn't know where he worked or lived. Tisha hadn't told me where she was living or working since she'd left the convent either, so I had no way to find her."

Crystal was clearly struggling with her story and I wanted to help, but I wasn't sure how to, so I just waited.

"Finally, about a month ago, Tisha called me. She said she'd lost her phone and hadn't received any of my calls, but she wanted me to attend her wedding, which was going to be held on Halloween. I told her I'd love to, but I insisted that I first meet the man she was going to marry. Eventually, she set up a dinner in Oahu. We met at a restaurant in Honolulu. I was somewhat disappointed that another couple had been invited to join us as well because it prevented me from asking a lot of questions, but I had to admit Ivan was charming. He was polite and attentive and seemed to be totally in to Tisha. I felt somewhat better after the dinner and agreed to attend the wedding."

"The other couple?" I asked.

"Lazarus and Lilith. That night everyone was dressed appropriately for the restaurant, so I wasn't aware at the time how deeply they were in to the whole Goth thing."

"I see. Go on."

"A week or so after that dinner I mentioned to a friend of mine who writes true crime books that my sister was getting married to a rich man on Halloween and that the wedding was being held over the weekend on a private island. She got a funny look on her face and asked the name of the groom. When I told her, she informed me that she'd looked into a cold case involving a man by that name who'd lived in Los Angeles but had moved to a private island he'd bought off Oahu. She asked me Ivan's last name and I realized Tisha had never told me what it was. I was of course interested in the details of the cold case, so my friend showed me her file on the mysterious death that had never been solved."

I was beginning to get a bad feeling. A really bad feeling.

"A woman named Gwyneth Morningstar had been found in an unmarked grave by a cadaver dog after a neighbor tipped off the police that she hadn't been seen in weeks, even though she'd had appointments and meetings she'd never shown up for. The neighbors insisted that was very uncharacteristic of the woman, so the police questioned the husband, Ivan Morningstar. He told the detectives he'd been out of town on business and his wife had gone to visit her sister. A call to the sister revealed that she hadn't spoken to Gwyneth in months and they'd had no plans for a visit. It took a bit of doing, but eventually the police gathered enough evidence to provide reasonable grounds and obtained a warrant to search the property. Mr. Morningstar had no idea what had happened to his wife and he had both receipts and eyewitnesses to prove he was, as he'd said, out of town at the time his wife was murdered. Charges were never brought against him and the case was filed away as unsolved."

I finally spoke. "You think Ivan Morningstar is Tisha's Ivan?"

"I wasn't sure at first. It seemed that the dead woman had strange symbols carved on her chest and Ivan Morningstar seemed to be a legitimate businessman, not a cult leader. Additionally, the photo of Ivan Morningstar my friend had on file didn't look a lot like the man I'd met at the restaurant, although there were some similarities. Tisha's Ivan has dark hair and dark eyes and Ivan Morningstar had blond hair and blue eyes. Ivan Morningstar was also a few pounds heavier than Tisha's Ivan, so he had a fuller face."

"Hair can be dyed, colored contacts worn, and weight lost," I pointed out.

"Exactly. I didn't have proof the two Ivans were the same, but I had my suspicions based on the fact that my friend's research revealed the Ivan who was suspected of his wife's murder had sold his Los Angeles estate and bought a private island near Oahu. The odds of the men not being the same were slim, so I called Tisha, and once again she began to ignore my calls. My friend had hit a dead end in her research of the case once Ivan Morningstar left Los Angeles, so I decided to see what I could dig up on my own." Crystal glanced at Cory. "Cory is a computer genius. He can find anything there is to find on the Web, even the deep Web. I asked him to poke around to see what he could find."

I looked directly at Cory. "So what have you found out? Can you prove Ivan Morningstar is the man Tisha is marrying?"

"We can't prove it, but we're fairly certain he is," Cory answered.

"Cory found out that Ivan and Gwyneth had been married on Halloween night ten years ago," Crystal informed us. Crystal's story had me on the edge of my seat, and

I could see Luke was just as fascinated. "We don't know exactly when Gwyneth died, but she was last seen on the morning of Halloween the year after she married Ivan Morningstar. According to what Cory has been able to find out, a friend took her out to breakfast to cheer her up when she shared that she was hurt and angry that her husband had gone off on a business trip on their first anniversary. She was never seen again. She had a dinner date that night with another friend that she didn't show up for. The coroner's report indicated that Gwyneth's body had some strange symbols carved into it, and it was suspected that she'd been killed as part of some sort of cult ritual, although the police never found any evidence to tie that theory to a specific cult, person, or group."

"Ivan and his Goth friends," I stated.

"I believe so," Cory spoke up. "But I have no proof. I found out this Ivan's legal last name is Bisbane, and he's a legitimate businessman who inherited a substantial amount of money from his mother and turned it into hundreds of millions of dollars by investing in all the right things at all the right times."

Crystal leaned forward and continued. "I know in my gut that the two Ivans are the same, but Cory wasn't able to find enough evidence to get the police involved. The photo of Ivan Morningstar isn't an exact match for Ivan Bisbane, and as of the time we boarded the boat to come here no laws had been broken. Tisha appears to be marrying Ivan willingly, and it isn't against the law to be a weirdo."

"So you came to rescue her after you realized she might be Ivan's next wife to die in an unexplained way," I said.

"I need to get her away from here. I've tried to talk to her, but I haven't managed to have even one minute alone with her since the day she told me she was engaged. When I met Tisha and Ivan for dinner that night I suggested that she accompany me to the bathroom in the hope of at least having a brief conversation with her, but Lilith immediately announced she needed to go as well and came with us."

"You seemed happy and appeared to be having a good time when we went dress shopping," I pointed out.

"I realized I had to make it seem as if I approved of the marriage and was happy for Tisha if I were ever to have any chance of getting her alone. The moment I set foot on this island and saw that weird castle I knew I'd been right about everything. My instinct is to grab her and run, but even if I could grab her there's nowhere to run to."

"With Dharma's death a murder has been committed. If we can contact the police that should give them reason enough to come out to the island and look around," I said.

"Sure, if we can get through to someone before my sister marries that monster."

"I have five brothers who are cops. If we can get a phone signal out one, or probably all of them, will come running."

"I'll try again as soon as the storm lets up," Luke promised.

Something occurred to me. "We left Dharma's body in the morgue. Cam, Luke, and I are the only ones to have seen it. You don't think Ivan would move it to cover up the crime, do you?"

There was a strange look on Luke's face. "If Crystal's theory is true and Ivan is marrying Tisha so that he can sacrifice her a year from now, I think hiding the body is exactly what he'd do."

Chapter 6

A wet trip to the mausoleum provided quite a surprise. Not only was Dharma's body gone but Cole's body was in the coffin, seemingly in her place. Like Dharma, he'd been shot through the chest and posed with his hands crossed over him.

"Okay, this is beyond strange," I whispered.

"Tell me about it," Crystal agreed. "Are you sure this is the coffin Dharma was in?"

I looked around the mausoleum. I was fairly sure it was the same coffin, but we decided to open all of them to be certain. The other coffins were empty.

If Ivan was behind this and his friends were backing him up, it would be their word against ours that Dharma had been shot and placed in the coffin in the first place. In fact, of the non-Goth guests, Luke, Cam, Kekoa, and I were the only ones to have even met the psychic. Buck and Bunny and Crystal and Cory all said they hadn't had the pleasure, yet none seemed to doubt our assertion that we had met her the previous afternoon and had found her dead that night.

"Now we have two mysteries," Cory stated. "The first is the disappearance of the body the four of you saw last night and the second is the new body that's been put in its place. Do you have any idea who might have done this?"

"I can think of a couple of people who might be responsible for Cole's death: Raven, who I haven't seen since last night but who seemed angry with him earlier in the day; Lazarus and/or Lilith, who Cole was seen arguing with on the beach. I have no idea who would have killed Dharma or had a reason to switch the bodies," I said.

"Who even knew about Dharma being dead?" Crystal asked.

"The only people we told last night were Buck and Bunny, and I don't think they're involved in this whole thing."

"Buck is Ivan's brother," Crystal pointed out.

"Yeah. But he said he hadn't seen Ivan in twenty years. In fact, he said he wouldn't even have come to the wedding except Tisha got hold of Bunny and convinced her that they should."

"I don't think we should share what we know with them," Crystal insisted.

"There's so much going on here that isn't what it seems."

I remembered again that Dharma had said something similar. I wondered if figuring out what that meant was the key to this whole thing.

"We told Lazarus, Lilith, Drusilla, and Damien about Dharma this morning," Luke pointed out. "None of them asked any questions or seemed surprised by our news. I'd be willing to bet that one of them—maybe *all* of them—is behind both the shooting of Dharma and the body being moved, although I have no idea whether they know Cole is dead."

"Here's what I don't get," I responded. "Say I'm the killer. I hit Cam and Kekoa over the head because they stumbled onto something they shouldn't have. I tie them up, take them to the mausoleum, and put them in coffins. Later, I shoot Dharma and place her in a coffin. At some point after that I move Dharma's body and put Cole in the coffin in her place. Why?"

Everyone was looking at me, but I could see they were still confused.

"It's Luke's opinion, and I agree with him, that whoever hit Cam and Kekoa over the head and put them in the coffins didn't intend to kill them. If they had, they'd most likely be dead."

"So you think whoever attacked them planned for them to either get out of the coffins on their own or to be found?" Crystal asked.

"That's what we think."

"But if the killer didn't want Dharma's body to be found why put her in the same place you'd put two others you *did* want to be found?" Cory continued.

"You're right; it makes no sense. Even if Luke and I hadn't found Cam and Kekoa, it seemed to us that eventually one of them would have woken up and realized the coffin wasn't locked and would have figured out a way to get out. The first thing either of them would have done was start opening coffins in search of the other and would almost certainly have found Dharma's body."

We all just looked at one another.

"Either Dharma's body was meant to be found or there are two bad guys," Luke concluded. "One who knocked out Cam and Kekoa and placed them in the coffins and another who shot Dharma and hid her body in one of the coffins without having any idea Cam and Kekoa were inside two others."

By this point my mind was totally blown. What in the heck had we gotten ourselves in to? Cults, murders, and cold case files. Yikes.

I looked around at the others, who appeared to be just as confused as I was. This whole thing really wasn't making sense. If the person who knocked Cam and Kekoa out didn't want them dead, why even put them in the coffins? Why not leave them on the beach or simply dump them inside the mausoleum? Why go to all the trouble of placing them in the coffins?

"How does Cole fit into all this and why switch out the bodies?" I asked.

No one had an answer.

"We should get back to the castle before someone misses us and wonders where we went," Crystal suggested. "We need to play it cool and act normal. If we start to act suspicious who knows what will happen? We are, after all, trapped on an island with at least one killer."

"Yeah, okay, you make a good point. Should we plan to meet again?" I asked.

"It's going to be hard until the rain stops," Cory said. "It's not like we can simply claim we're going for a stroll."

"If someone finds something important we'll slip a note to the others and take it from there. In the meantime, keep your eyes open," Crystal said.

We decided we shouldn't all go back to the castle at the same time in the event anyone was watching, so Luke and I headed there first. Crystal and Cory planned to wait a half hour before following us.

When we got back we went upstairs to fill Cam and Kekoa in on the latest developments, and then the four of us went downstairs to present an appearance of normalcy. I hoped Tisha would be there, but she wasn't. If I'd wanted to speak to her alone before our discussion with Crystal, I really wanted to now. Sometime during the course of the day I realized the reason she'd invited Buck and Bunny and Kekoa and me to her wedding must have been because she'd realized she was in trouble and hoped one or all of us could save her before it was too late.

Buck and Bunny were seated at the dining table playing a card game when we entered the room. It didn't appear anyone else was around. Crystal had warned us not to share what we knew with them, but it would seem odd not to talk to them about what had happened considering the fact that Buck had helped us out the previous night. Besides, I wanted to ask Buck what he knew about Ivan. I needed a few minutes to gather my thoughts, so I decided to engage in idle chitchat until I found the right opening.

"I was wondering where the four of you had gone off to," Buck greeted us.

"After the late night we had we slept in," I explained as I sat down at the table with the friendly couple.

"How are you both feeling?" Bunny asked Kekoa and Cam after they sat down as well.

"Better, thank you," Kekoa answered for both of them.

"I will say you gave me quite a scare," Bunny commented. "I'm glad you've recovered from your ordeal."

"Speaking of which," Buck said, "have you figured out who might have done that to you?"

"We still don't know anything," I shared. "Luke and I got up for coffee before returning to bed and we told Drusilla, Damien, Lazarus, and Lilith what happened, but I haven't seen the others."

"We haven't either," Bunny confirmed. "The place was deserted when Buck and I came downstairs this morning and we hadn't seen a soul until the four of you came in. I must say this entire situation has me feeling unsettled."

"Something is definitely up," Buck said. "Something I don't like one bit, and I intend to find out what exactly it is."

"Have the four of you eaten?" Bunny asked. "Someone—I imagine the cook—left sandwiches in the refrigerator and soup in a pot. It's actually quite good."

"I could eat," Cam answered.

"Yeah, me too," Luke seconded.

"Why don't you all go and pick out what you want and bring it back to the table? Buck and I will stay to chat with you while you eat," Bunny suggested.

As soon as the four of us went into the kitchen Kekoa pulled me aside. "What now?" she whispered. "You said not to trust them, but he's the one who stitched me up. I can't be rude to him."

"We'll talk to him about what the four of us know, but we won't bring up the rest. Personally, I trust Buck, but Crystal isn't comfortable sharing everything with him, and it's her sister whose life is on the line."

"I'll just nod and let you do the talking," Kekoa decided.

"That sounds like a good plan. Remember, as far as they know we don't know Dharma's body is missing or that Cole is dead, so no one bring it up unless one of them does."

Everyone muttered their agreement.

"And nothing at all about the cold case file," I added. "We need to play this very carefully if we want to get off the island alive."

"Maybe once we finish lunch we should go into the media room and watch a movie until it's time for dinner," Luke suggested. "We're less likely to get ourselves into trouble if we don't speak to anyone."

"Good idea." Cam nodded.

The movie idea had merit, but what I really wanted to do was find out what was behind all the locked doors in the castle. If only I could track down a key with no one knowing, I might be able to snoop around without anyone being the wiser.

Buck and Bunny were talking about the fact that the castle appeared to be deserted when we returned to the dining table. They said they'd assumed that because we'd been invited to spend four days on the island there would be four days' worth of planned activities. Sure, a murder could put a damper on the festivities, but at this point we didn't even know for certain that the bride and groom were aware of what had occurred.

"I wonder if we should try to track down some of the household staff," Bunny said. "Surely they would know how to get hold of Ivan in the event of an emergency."

"Have you seen any of the staff since you've been downstairs?" I asked.

"No. Not a one."

"The cook, Mrs. Baker, was in the kitchen earlier, but I have no idea where she went after that," Luke shared. "I suppose we could all look around after we eat."

"I'm beginning to wish I'd never let that girl of Ivan's talk me into coming here," Bunny commented.

"How exactly did she convince you?" I asked. "It really was a long way for you to come."

"I guess she appealed to my curiosity and my strong sense of family. I always knew Buck had a brother, but I'd never met him and Buck never talked about him, so I wondered."

"I never talked about him because there was nothing to say. Like I told you before, I don't know Ivan very well," Buck defended himself.

"Yes, and I can see it might have been for the best to leave things alone, but at the time she called I didn't know about the whole Dracula thing. What I knew was someone who seemed like a lovely young woman had made the effort to reach out to let us know that Buck's brother was getting married and that it was important to both of them that we attend their wedding. I'd always wanted to meet Ivan, so I agreed to Morticia's request and made the airline reservations that same day."

"And when was that?" I asked.

"I guess it was a month or so ago."

"And had you spoken to either Ivan or Morticia since then?"

"No. I received directions to the boat shuttle in the mail a couple of weeks after the phone call, but I didn't speak to the future Mrs. Drysdale again."

"Mrs. Drysdale?"

"I guess I assume Ivan's bride will take his name, but in this day and age who knows?"

"Ivan's last name is Drysdale?" I clarified.

"It was our father's name, it's mine, and it would be Ivan's unless he changed it," Buck chimed in. "Which is possible because our mother left with him when he was only two years old."

"That's true," Bunny acknowledged. "I suppose your mother could have gone back to her maiden name and changed Ivan's name as well."

"And your mother's maiden name was…?" I asked.

"Wilcox."

So while Bisbane might be the name Ivan was currently using, it wasn't his birth name. Interesting.

"I don't mean to be nosy, but under the circumstance I find I'm curious about Ivan's childhood. Did you ever see each other after your mother left with him?" I asked.

"Every now and then. My mother was a very controlling woman. She was very different from my father, who was a strong man but had a gentle way about him. Ivan is ten years younger than me, so it was only the three of us for quite some time, and while it pains me to say it, I don't think my mother really liked me."

"Didn't like you?" Kekoa gasped. "How could a mother not like her own son?"

"I take after my father in looks and personality, and although they were married, I don't think my mother liked my father much either. Ours wasn't a happy family, so I was shocked, as was pretty much everyone we knew, when my mother became pregnant shortly after my tenth birthday. It was obvious Ivan took hold of my mother's heart in a way I never did. She doted on him twenty-four hours a day."

"Twenty-four hours a day?" I asked.

"My father and mother had been sleeping in separate rooms for years by the time Ivan was born. When she found out she was pregnant she set up a crib in her room and it was in that crib Ivan slept until she took him and moved out of our lives."

I looked around the table. I was willing to bet that everyone was thinking the same thing. Buck's father was most likely not Ivan's biological father. I really hated to blurt out such a sensitive thing, so I decided to glide on over it.

"And after your mother left, did you see her again?"

I wasn't expecting Buck to answer my question, and I certainly didn't expect him to open up to a room full of complete strangers, but the situation in which we found ourselves had created a sort of intimacy that seemed to compel him to make us understand exactly where he fit into this unusual affair.

"A couple of times. I was twelve, almost thirteen, when she left, and while I was hurt that she would simply walk out of my life, I had my own things going on, the way teens do. I had school and my work at the ranch as well as friends, clubs, sports." Buck glanced at Bunny, who nodded, as if encouraging him to continue.

It was odd seeing this large, confident man looking so vulnerable.

"When I was fourteen my mother arranged for me to spend a couple of weeks in Los Angeles. It was the worst two weeks of my life. Not only did the big city make my skin itch with all the noise, people, and pollution, but my annoying little brother decided he wanted to follow me everywhere I went, and I was forced to endure his presence for what seemed like endless days of answering every question beginning with the word *why* known to man."

I smiled. I remembered when my niece and nephew were in the *why* stage.

"After that I saw him a couple of times for a day or two at a time. When I was twenty-five I was in almost constant conflict with my dad over how to run the ranch, so I decided to join the army. I found myself feeling sentimental, I guess, right before I left Texas, so I made the trip west for a few days. Ivan was fifteen and into his own things, so that visit didn't go well either."

"His own things?" I asked.

"The occult, monsters, witchcraft. I assumed it was a teen fad that he'd outgrow. I had no idea what I was walking into until I arrived."

"And how long ago was that?"

"Twenty years. I never saw him or spoke to him after that until yesterday." Buck shrugged sheepishly. "Why am I telling you all this again?"

"Because I asked, and it could be important. Ivan is obviously a unique individual. He's smart and sophisticated on one hand, but he's so deeply enmeshed in his fantasy world that he's spent millions of dollars creating a place where he is in fact an unholy prince. I find that both terrifying and fascinating."

"Do you think we're in danger?" Bunny asked me.

"I don't know," I said honestly.

Chapter 7

After lunch Buck and Bunny decided to join us in the media room for the movie. I think we were all feeling unsettled with everything that was going on and there seemed to be comfort in numbers. The movie was kind of a blur as I found myself unable to concentrate, but I did enjoy sitting with Luke in the dark theater, watching a comedy that didn't seem to have a plot but was funny nonetheless.

When the movie was over Buck and Bunny returned to their room and Luke, Cam, Kekoa, and I went upstairs to the room Kekoa and I were sharing. The rain had stopped at least temporarily, and the sky had cleared somewhat, although there were more clouds on the horizon.

"That's odd," Luke commented.

"What's odd?'

"The sky is clear, at least for the moment, but my satellite phone still won't work. I thought for sure it was the storm blocking the signal."

"Did it work when we first got here? Before the clouds rolled in?"

"I didn't need to make a call, so I didn't even think to check. I think I'm going to go down to the beach where there are no trees or buildings and try it there."

"I'll come with you," I offered.

I looked at Cam and Kekoa.

"I'd love to lie down for a bit before dinner," Kekoa answered. "I'm feeling a little headachy."

"I'll stay with her," Cam said.

"Be careful," Kekoa cautioned us before we left the room.

"We will," I assured her.

The air felt heavy from all the moisture, but the sun was already low in the sky and the temperature remained well below average, so it was actually a pleasant afternoon. Luke and I walked hand in hand as we navigated the minefield of debris that had been left by the storm. I hoped the gardens hadn't been destroyed. It seemed as if the wind and rain had approached hurricane velocity a few time during the past twelve hours.

The beach was covered with litter but otherwise deserted when Luke and I arrived. He tried his satellite phone from several different locations but still couldn't get a signal.

"I'm not familiar with satellite phones. Do they normally work this far from civilization?"

"They work pretty much anywhere as long as the satellite signal isn't interrupted. I should be able to get one out here, although I suppose, depending on the placement of the satellite, those cliffs to the left of us could be interfering with the signal." Luke looked around. "I'm going to see if I can get higher."

"The trail Mr. Graves pointed out supposedly wound up the mountain to the waterfall. Let's try that," I suggested.

Although the sun was low in the sky we still had several hours of light, so Luke and I started up the steep, muddy trail. As we hiked in single file I could see we weren't going to be able to make it to the top of the mountain and back down again before it got dark; traversing the trail was slow going with the slippery mud that seemed to cause us to slide down a step for every two we traveled upward.

"Maybe we should try this again tomorrow," Luke said after thirty minutes with little progress.

"Yeah, I was thinking the same thing. It looks like the trail levels off just up ahead for a bit. I can hear the sound of water. Maybe it's the falls. Let's check."

Luke didn't answer, but he did fall into line behind me as I made my way toward the clearing ahead. When we arrived at the clearing we found not the falls but a large clear-water lake. On the opposite shore of the lake was a small structure that looked a lot like an enclosed gazebo. The trail continued up the mountain to the left and there were sheer cliffs to the right, so I couldn't immediately figure out how anyone was supposed to access the small building.

"It really is beautiful," I said.

"It really is." Luke held the phone up in the air and walked around in a circle. "I'm still not getting anything. I wonder if Ivan has blocked the signal for some reason."

"I wouldn't be at all surprised," I mumbled.

"I'm going to climb up onto those rocks over there to see if I can pick up the signal there."

"Okay," I answered as I knelt down at water's edge and used my hands to splash cool water on my face. I was seriously considering a swim when I saw a flash of white out of the corner of my eye. I stood up and looked across the lake. The opposite shore was far enough off that it was impossible to pick up any detail, but it looked like someone dressed in white was standing there.

"Luke," I yelled.

"Yeah?" he yelled back.

"Did you see that? Across the lake? It looks like Dharma."

Luke looked in the direction I was pointing. "I don't see anything. Besides, Dharma is dead, remember?"

I stood perfectly still as I willed the figure I'd seen for just a split second to make a reappearance. It was true Dharma was dead, and it was also true shadows often did weird things when the sun was low in the sky, but I was certain the image I'd seen wasn't a shadow but the woman who'd died the previous night.

"I'm going to go check."

Luke started back toward me. "Check? How? It would take hours to walk around this lake with the terrain the way it is."

I pulled off my shoes. "I'm going to swim."

"Swim? It must be a good mile across. Maybe more."

I turned and looked at Luke, who had reached my side by now. "Don't worry. I'm a lifeguard, remember? A mile is nothing. I'll try to hurry."

I dove into the water and swam as fast as I could toward the other shore.

There's something about the absolute silence that can be found in the water that makes you feel alone in the universe. In the beginning you experience a burst of adrenaline as your muscles jump into action, but once you find your breath and your rhythm, effort fades and all that's left is the synchronicity of your strokes as they form a symphony with the water. I'd found a home in the water when I was just a small child, and in many ways it's the water where I still feel the most comfortable.

I let my thoughts roam as I swam toward the opposite shore; the dreams I had, the plans I'd made. My life's plan to this point had been clearly defined. Like my father and my five brothers, I knew it was my destiny to be a cop; ever since I was old enough to have dreams, every move I'd made, every decision that had been necessary, had been focused solely on achieving that single undeniable outcome. I knew in my heart I was born to be a cop, an everyday hero who laughed in the face of danger, but as I swam toward an image that clearly couldn't exist, I struggled with an emotion that didn't have a place in the mind of an everyday hero: fear.

I paused on the opposite shore to wipe the water from my eyes. I'd seen the flash of white near the edge of the forest. I supposed it could have been a trick of the light, but somehow I knew finding out what had happened to Dharma would provide us with the answers we needed. Of course now that I was here I really had no idea where to start looking, so I headed toward the structure I'd seen from the opposite side of the lake.

"Oz," I greeted the older man, who was kneeling at an altar. "I'm sorry if I've disturbed you."

"I was expecting you. Please have a seat." Oz motioned toward a bench that had been placed nearby.

"You were expecting me?"

Oz just smiled.

I sat down on the bench and wondered how to proceed. "I'm sorry about Dharma," I began. "I know you were friends."

I began to squirm when Oz still didn't speak.

"I know this is going to sound crazy with Dharma's death and all, but I was on the opposite shore with Luke and I swore I saw Dharma down by the water. I know that isn't possible. Is it? Of course it isn't. Dharma is dead. I saw her. We saw her."

Oz sat down next to me. "What is it you think you know about Dharma's fate?"

"Something happened last night. I heard a shot." I thought of Luke. "*We* heard a shot while we were looking for our friends. We saw Drusilla walking from the forest trail, so we followed her. She suggested that we look for our friends in the mausoleum and we did. They had been knocked out and placed in coffins. In the process of looking for them we found Dharma. She'd been shot."

"And then?"

"And then Luke and I took Kekoa and Cam back to the house."

"And Dharma?"

"We didn't go back for her. Maybe we should have, but she was already dead. There was nothing we could do. When we got to the house we woke Buck, who stitched up Kekoa's head. We sat with her and Cam for most of the night to make sure they were going to be okay. When we returned to the mausoleum today Dharma was gone. Did you move her body?"

"Dharma is where she is meant to be."

"Okay. Good. I think." I was quiet for a moment and then said, "I don't suppose you know who shot Cole? We found him in the mausoleum this morning."

"I know not of that which does not concern me."

"I see," I said, although I really didn't see at all. Oz was such an odd man, so I decided to change the subject. "Do you live here?" I looked around the small building. It didn't look as if anyone could live in a gazebo, but Oz didn't look physically capable of either swimming across the lake or hiking the cliff trail, so I had to wonder how he'd gotten here.

"I live many places and no place."

"I wasn't sure when I met you if you were of native blood. You said you were here to perform a blessing. Are you a witch doctor of some sort?"

"It is late. You should start back before the darkness comes."

"Yes," I said, even though my question hadn't been answered. "I guess I should." I stood up. "Are you okay here by yourself? Can I help you in some way?"

"I am where I am meant to be."

I leaned forward and hugged Oz. He felt good and solid, so at least I knew he wasn't a figment of my imagination or a spirit of some sort. "I'm sorry again about Dharma." I turned and headed back toward the water. When I stood at the edge of the lake I turned and looked back for a moment before diving in. Dharma, or someone who looked like her, was standing at the edge of the forest. Her image was there for just a second before it disappeared. Maybe I was seeing Dharma's ghost or maybe I was hallucinating. I looked one last time before diving into the deep blue water. I'd need to make good time to arrive at the other shore before sunset, so I cleared my mind and focused on the rhythm of my breathing and my strokes.

Luke was pacing back and forth along the beach when I arrived at the opposite shore.

"Thank goodness you're back. It'll be dark soon. Did you find what you were looking for?"

"I don't know. I saw something, but it was just a flash. It could have been a shadow or a hallucination. It could even have been a ghost, but I've been thinking about it. I think Dharma is alive."

Luke frowned. "Alive? We both saw her. She was dead."

"Was she?" I sat down on a rock to put my shoes back on so we could begin our trek down the mountain before it became totally dark. "We heard a shot when we were looking for Cam and Kekoa. When we arrived at the mausoleum we immediately heard Cam and went directly to the coffin and rescued him. We then realized Kekoa must also be in a coffin and started opening lids. I opened the lid of the coffin where Dharma was lying. She had a trail of blood running from her chest. We realized she must have been the victim of the shot we'd heard and frantically got back to looking for Kekoa. Once we found her we went back to the castle and didn't return to the mausoleum until this morning. When we looked for Dharma's body it was missing."

"So you're saying she wasn't dead?" Luke seemed to begin to catch on as we started down the steep path.

"I never checked for a pulse; did you?"

"No," Luke admitted. "As soon as I realized she'd been murdered all I could think about was finding Kekoa."

"Same here."

"She *looked* dead."

"I agree. But did she look dead because she actually was, or did she look dead because we heard a shot, found a body covered in a red fluid in a coffin, and our minds filled in the rest?"

Luke grabbed my elbow as I slipped on a patch of mud. "You think it was all staged?"

"Maybe. I don't know for sure, but what I do know is that I saw a woman on the opposite shore of the lake who looked exactly like Dharma and Oz wasn't at all grieving over his friend's death."

"Oz was on the other side of the lake?"

"He was in the gazebo."

"Was he alone? How did he get there?"

"He seemed to be alone, but I have no idea how he got there. Maybe there's an easier way we don't know about."

Luke fell into silence as we navigated a particularly treacherous stretch of the trail.

"Why in the world would anyone stage a murder?" Luke eventually asked.

I shrugged. "Nothing has made sense since we landed on this creepy island. Did you have any luck getting a satellite signal while I was swimming across the lake?"

"No. I'm convinced Ivan is jamming the signal. Now that the storm has passed, I can't see any other reason why I can't find at least a weak link. If you believe Dharma's death was staged do you think Cole's was also?"

Did I? Cole certainly looked dead, but once again we hadn't checked for a pulse. "I'm not sure. Let's go back to the mausoleum to check."

Luke and I hiked in silence, each lost in our own thoughts as we hurried to beat the darkness. I suppose we should have taken the time to go back to the castle for flashlights.

"Do you remember when we were speaking to Oz and Dharma yesterday by the pool?" I eventually said.

"Yeah."

"She told me not to trust what I saw. Do you think all the weird stuff that's been happening is an intentional illusion to distract us from what's really going on here?"

"What do you mean?"

"At first I couldn't figure out why Tisha would invite two un-Goth friends to her Goth wedding, but then I began to suspect she might have realized she was in a sticky situation and wanted us to rescue her. As recently as twenty-four hours ago, I was focused on that and that alone, but then Cam and Kekoa were attacked and Dharma was murdered—or at least we thought she was murdered—and I got completely distracted."

"So if Dharma isn't dead and her body was staged to distract us, does that mean she's in on whatever is going on?"

Did it? It would make sense that she would be, but somehow that didn't fit either. "I don't know. Maybe she was drugged or maybe she really is dead and my mind is playing tricks on me. All I do know is that we need to figure out a way to get Tisha alone, and then we need to get her, along with Crystal and Cory, Buck and Bunny, and Cam and Kekoa off this island."

"What about Oz? And Dharma, if, as you suspect, she isn't really dead?"

"I have a feeling they can take care of themselves."

When we got to the mausoleum we found that, like Dharma's body, Cole's was missing. I didn't know what was going on, but I knew I didn't like it. "We need to get off this island."

"Yeah," Luke said. "We really do."

Back at the castle, Buck, Bunny, Cam, Kekoa, Crystal, and Cory were sitting at the dining room table. We didn't see anyone else.

"What happened to you?" Cam asked as we left a trail of mud behind us.

"We went for a hike. It was muddy," I explained. "Where is everyone?"

"When we came down there was a buffet dinner set out on the sideboard. The cook told us to help ourselves because the others had been delayed," Bunny, who was formally dressed for dinner, told us.

"Delayed?" I asked. "Delayed how?"

"We don't have any idea," Crystal answered. "I'm not even sure if *delayed* means they'll be down later or they won't be down at all."

I looked down at my damp, muddy clothes. "Luke and I need to shower and change. I have interesting news I'd like to share when I get back."

"News?" Kekoa asked. "What kind of news?"

"Shower first and news later," I said as I headed for the stairs, with Luke trailing along behind me.

The warm water from the shower felt good on my weary muscles. Between only getting a few hours of sleep the previous night, the stress, and the two-mile swim at top speed, I wasn't ashamed to admit feeling weary. Maybe I'd turn in early if there were no more vicious attacks, bodies in coffins, or cold case mysteries to deal with.

I thought about the story Crystal had shared with us. Could Ivan have killed his first wife? And if so, was he planning to kill Tisha? I had to wonder if there had been others. According to Crystal, the murder seemed to be linked to some sort of ritual. If that was true and Gwyneth had been killed nine years ago could there have been others in the interim we didn't know about? I wished we had access to a computer. Luke had brought his laptop, but we'd been unable to get Internet access.

As I ran conditioner through my hair, I realized how odd it was that Ivan didn't have Wi-Fi access. He was a businessman after all. He kept his office door locked, which wasn't all that strange, but it stood to reason that if it was possible to get inside there would be a computer hooked up to the Web. Of course he might just have his computers stashed somewhere on the top floors of the castle. The place was huge and we'd only seen a portion of it.

I turned off the water and grabbed a towel from the rack. A black towel. I like black and wear it often myself when heat isn't a factor, but after the dark, dank weekend we'd been having I thought I'd stick to bright colors for a while.

I dried off, wrapped the towel around my body, and went out into the bedroom. I opened my suitcase and was searching for a clean pair of shorts when I heard voices in the hall.

"The witch and her voodoo priest sidekick are gone and Cole is missing as well. The guests seem suspicious, and the girl has a definite look of fear in her eyes. This whole thing is falling apart. We need to act and we need to act now."

"Not until the witching hour."

I continued to listen, but the voices had moved on. It was now even more imperative that we acted fast.

Chapter 8

Luke had already joined the others when I returned to the dining room table. There were somber looks on the faces of everyone there, which wasn't surprising; we were all coming to the realization that we were trapped in a horror movie with no clear means of escape.

"We need to come up with a plan to get off this island," Bunny cried, fear evident in her voice. "I try to have an open mind and I realize not everyone who embraces the Goth side is evil, but there are just too many odd things going on for me to feel comfortable."

Crystal lowered her voice and leaned in closer. "Yes, we need to get off the island, but not without my sister."

"Are you sure she isn't part of whatever is going on?" Buck asked.

"I'm sure," Crystal said with conviction. "Tisha has made some bad choices in her life, but she's a good person. A kind person. There's no way she'd be part of something that brought harm to others."

I could see Crystal was uncomfortable having this conversation in front of Buck and Bunny. I didn't blame her. There was no way to know for certain whether he would defend his brother, though I had the sense that Buck didn't necessarily look at Ivan fondly but more as someone he didn't know and had no desire to get close to.

Buck turned me. "You said you had news?"

I'd promised Crystal I wouldn't tell Buck anything she'd provided about the cold case and I wouldn't, but Buck and Bunny already knew about Dharma's death and the strange events surrounding it, so I didn't see a problem with sharing my news about Dharma and Cole, and perhaps getting Buck to talk about his relationship with Ivan with Crystal and Cory.

"Why don't we all go for a walk?" I suggested. "The storm has passed and it's actually a pretty nice evening."

Crystal glanced at me and I nodded in an attempt to assure her that I would only share my news, not hers.

"I don't have shoes for walking," Bunny said.

"Then maybe we can just sit at one of the tables on the patio. It seems a shame to waste such a beautiful evening."

"Well, okay, I guess that will be all right."

"I'll grab a bottle of whiskey from the bar and some glasses," Buck offered.

"None for me," I said. The last thing I needed was to have a foggy head brought about by too much alcohol.

As soon as we were gathered around a table near the pool, I filled them in on my maybe sighting of Dharma; the fact that her body had been missing that morning, replaced by Cole's; and that when we'd gone by the mausoleum later in the afternoon Cole's body had been missing as well. I admitted that my vision of Dharma could have been an illusion, but I also pointed out that no one had checked for a pulse or confirmed that she was really dead.

"I did just take your word for it that a woman named Dharma even existed and had been murdered," Buck responded. "What about Cole? Do we think he was really dead?"

"I don't know about Cole, but with Dharma it all happened so fast," Cam contributed. "Lani found the body, which intensified our fear that Kekoa could be dead, and we all focused our energy on finding her and getting her back to the castle."

"You really think it's possible the death was staged?" Kekoa asked.

"I don't know. I suppose she might have been dead, as I'd originally thought, and what I saw at the lake was only an illusion. She certainly looked dead; the wound in her chest looked very real. I don't know if Cole and Dharma are alive or dead, but there's definitely something other than a normal wedding going on, and I have a feeling our presence here has to do with more than just participating in the happy event."

I looked at Buck. "I know Ivan is your brother, but you've admitted you don't really know him. Do you think it's possible he could be behind all the strange goings-on?"

Buck shook his head. "I have no idea. As I told you earlier, I hadn't had any contact with Ivan in twenty years and I didn't know him well before that. He was an odd child. My mother doted on him, and I guess that made me jealous at first, but as Ivan got older and my mother's obsession with him increased, I found myself being happy I'd dodged a bullet."

"Obsession?" I asked. That seemed like a strange word to use to describe the relationship between a mother and son.

"From the time Ivan was born our mother was always with him. She'd put a crib in her room when he was an infant, but I noticed that most of the time he slept in her bed rather than in his own. She took him to Los Angeles when he was only two, and maybe it isn't all that weird for a two-year-old to sleep with his mother, but I don't think that ended when they left the ranch."

I hated to even ask but knew I should. "Do you think there was anything inappropriate going on?"

Buck got a troubled look on his face. "If you're hinting at an incestuous relationship, no, I don't think so. I think my mom just bonded with him in a way that wasn't entirely natural. It seemed as if he became the most important thing in her life, and she was probably the most important thing in his."

"Is your mother still alive?"

"No. She died in her sleep eleven years ago. I wouldn't have even known about it, but my mother's attorney notified my father and he told me. It seemed Mother's death was quite sudden and Ivan didn't deal with it very well. He chose not to have a funeral so I didn't make the trip west, but I heard he left home shortly after that and wasn't seen for almost a year."

I did some quick math and realized if Buck's brother was really Ivan Morningstar he had married Gwyneth within a year of his mother's death. I wondered if Buck knew about that.

"Do you know if Ivan was married before this?"

Crystal glared at me.

"I have absolutely no idea. He could have a harem stashed away for all I know. He was just a kid the last time I saw him, and like I've said many times, we didn't keep in touch."

Bunny put her hand on Buck's arm. "I'm sorry I forced the issue about us coming here. Ivan's fiancée seemed so nice on the phone and I really wanted to meet your family, or at least what's left of it. Now look at the mess we're in."

Buck patted Bunny's hand. "Don't worry. It'll be fine. We'll get off this island one way or another."

I looked at Luke. "I've been thinking about the fact that we're on an isolated island with no means of transportation or communication. That makes no sense. Sure, the boat shuttle left, but Ivan must have a private boat and most likely a helicopter."

"I agree."

"And he must also have Internet as well as phone access. I know you believe your signal is blocked, but Ivan must have a different one for his own use."

"I'm not sure about the phone signal, but there's most likely a satellite dish on the island somewhere to provide internet access," Luke said.

"We need to get a look at the rooms that are currently behind locked doors," I asserted. "Ivan's office, the wings of the castle that extend beyond the main living area, the uppermost floors."

"I'm pretty good at picking locks," Cory offered.

"If we start snooping around someone will notice," Bunny worried.

"Yeah, that's a possibility." I nodded. "Especially if there are security cameras."

"Why don't we focus on finding a means of transportation first?" Buck suggested. "If there's a helicopter or boat it won't be located on the castle grounds. Once we find a mode of transportation we can concentrate on finding Crystal's sister."

I looked up at the sky. Bright stars shone overhead. Hopefully tomorrow would be rain free and we could look around under the guise of taking a hike.

"Okay, let's meet up at breakfast tomorrow," I said. "We have to remember to be careful about being overheard when we're indoors. The others seem to have disappeared, but I heard two people talking in the hall outside my room when I was getting changed, so they're around somewhere."

"We should probably go back inside in small groups or pairs," Crystal suggested.

"Bunny and I will go first," Buck offered. "We'll see you all at breakfast."

When they'd gone Crystal turned to me. "Are you sure we can trust them?"

"I'm not sure about trusting anyone or anything on this island, including my own eyes, but yeah, my sense is that Buck's telling the truth and he's a pawn in whatever game is being played the same as we are."

"He stitched up my head, which makes me like him," Kekoa added.

"The story that Tisha called Bunny and convinced her to come here tracks," I added. "Tisha invited Kekoa and me to the wedding out of the blue as well. I didn't know why then, and I still don't to a certain degree, but maybe she knew she was in trouble and wanted to be sure there were going to be people on the island who would help her."

"Or maybe Tisha is in on it and she invited us here to serve as some sort of sacrifice for the Dracula wannabes," Cam countered.

"She wouldn't do that," Crystal insisted.

"I agree, she wouldn't," I said, supporting Crystal's assertion. "But we know there's something going on. As I said, when I was getting dressed after my shower I overheard someone talking in the hall. They said something about needing to act now because the guests were getting suspicious."

"*Act now*? What could that mean?" Cam asked.

"I have no idea. But the other person said they needed to wait until the witching hour. Does anyone know what time that is?"

"I would think midnight," Luke said.

"Or midnight on Halloween, to be specific," Cory added.

"Or it could be a sacred time specific to the belief of whatever demon these people worship," Cam speculated.

"We're supposed to be staying on the island until Tuesday morning, so whenever it is, it will happen between now and then," I stated firmly.

"I think Cam and I will go up next," Kekoa informed us. "My head has been pounding for the past hour and all this talk about sacrifices is seriously creeping me out."

"Okay, I'll be up soon," I promised her.

"I'll stay with Kekoa until you come," Cam offered. "I don't think it's a good idea for any of us to be alone."

"Okay. I won't be long."

Crystal crossed her legs up under her body and rested her elbows on them. Then she put her head in her hands and looked at the ground.

"Are you okay?" Cory asked.

"No, I'm not okay. My sister is engaged to Dracula, who probably has short- or long-term plans to kill her, and I can't get two minutes alone with her to warn her."

"Ivan's first wife didn't die until her one-year wedding anniversary, which gives us a year to save her even if the marriage does happen." I tried, probably unsuccessfully, to comfort her.

"Ivan is controlling Tisha and I feel so helpless."

"I know. Although, if that's true and Tisha invited us against his wishes, why didn't he just uninvite us?" I wondered.

"Maybe he needs her to marry him willingly, or maybe he really does need bodies to sacrifice," Cory speculated.

"Maybe, but we might just be letting our imaginations get away from us." I took a deep breath and decided to take a step back from the panic I was feeling. "We know the eight of us who aren't part of Ivan's Goth group were invited by Tisha. We suspect she may not be marrying him willingly, but we don't know that for certain because we haven't been able to speak to her. The fact that a group of friends all wear black and have tattoos and piercings has led us to a discussion about human sacrifice and satanic rituals. Maybe we're getting ahead of ourselves."

"What about Cam and Kekoa?" Crystal asked. "They actually were assaulted and left in coffins."

"Yeah, that's admittedly strange," I had to agree.

"And this Dharma you've been telling us about was either shot and put into a coffin or she was part of the staging of a murder, as was the somewhat strange Cole," Cory added. "Either way creepy."

"I guess I'm trying too hard to convince myself we're overreacting; obviously we aren't. I think I'm going to take a walk to clear my head."

"That's what the next victim says in every horror movie I've ever seen," Crystal pointed out.

"True. But I'll be careful."

"I'll go with you." Luke offered.

"I think Cory and I will go up. We'll see you at breakfast."

Crystal and Cory left, and Luke and I decided to walk through the garden. It was illuminated with solar lights and was still close enough to the castle that we would most likely not be ambushed and stashed into coffins as Cam and Kekoa had been, and I was interested in how it had fared during the storm. It was a warm and balmy night and the wind had died down, leaving behind a feeling of stagnation in its wake.

"When Tisha invited me to a wedding on a private island I was picturing a lot more romance and a lot less death and conspiracy." I rested my head on Luke's shoulder as we walked hand in hand.

"This weekend has been unusual, although my life in general seems to have taken a turn toward the absurd ever since I helped you investigate that first murder."

"Do you ever wish you hadn't gotten involved?"

Luke stopped walking. He pulled me into his arms and looked me in the eye. "Not for one minute. Things have become a bit unpredictable and chaotic since I became involved with you and your friends, but I wouldn't change a single thing."

I wrapped my arms around his neck, stood on tiptoe, and kissed him on the lips. He lifted me so that my feet were off the ground as he deepened the kiss.

Chapter 9

Sunday, October 30

The kitchen and dining room were completely deserted the next morning except for Mrs. Baker, who was serving the food, and Buck and Bunny, Cory and Crystal, Cam and Kekoa, and Luke and me,

"Are the others going to be down?" I asked the cook.

"Today is a day of fasting. I'll be retreating to my room as well. I've left salads and sandwiches in the refrigerator as well as casseroles that can be heated and fresh-baked goods in the pantry. Feel free to eat whatever you choose at your leisure."

"Are you fasting as well?" I asked.

"No, but it's the master's wish that his friends and staff honor the day of fasting and prayer as he does."

I frowned. *The master*?

It didn't seem as if we were expected to fast, which was good because I was starving, but it did seem odd that everyone other than the eight of us was required to participate in the day of isolation. I tried not to let my imagination run free, but I felt a bit like a pig being fattened for slaughter.

"Before you go, can you tell me how to get hold of you or one of our hosts should there be an emergency or we have a question?"

"I'm afraid you'll be on your own. The others are sequestered in another wing of the castle and I plan to lock myself in my room. Have a nice day." She turned and left the room.

Okay, that was strange, but no stranger than anything else that had happened since we arrived on the island. When I joined the others at the table I filled them in on my conversation with the cook.

"It's probably a good thing they won't be underfoot," Buck commented.

"Yeah, I guess."

"Do we have a plan?" Cory asked.

I looked around the room. Just because they weren't around didn't mean they couldn't listen in. "Luke and I are planning to go for a hike. Would you all care to join us?"

Crystal gave the others a meaningful look before saying she'd love to. After a bit of discussion we decided to take our breakfast outdoors as well. At least we'd be able to speak freely. Or I hoped we could. There was no telling where a listening device might be planted.

"I think we should split up today," I suggested after we gathered around a table by the pool. "This is a big island and we can cover more territory if we head in a couple of different directions."

"I don't think Kekoa should strain herself," Cam said.

"I'm fine."

"Maybe, but the terrain is pretty rough once you leave the grounds surrounding the castle."

"I agree with Cam," I said. I looked at Bunny, who didn't appear to be in the sort of physical shape to take on a strenuous hike. "Bunny should probably stay behind as well."

"I'm not staying alone," Bunny countered.

"Cam, you stay with Kekoa and Bunny. I know you're feeling better, but Buck has army training that could come in handy. I know I said we should split up, but I'm reconsidering that. We all have different talents, and because we don't know which skill set will come in handy I say we stay together."

"You should take water," Kekoa offered.

"And flashlights," Cam added.

"I have a backpack I normally use as a purse. It's in my room. I'll get it and load it up and then we'll be on our way. Hopefully we'll find some mode of transportation and then all we'll have to do is figure out how to snag Tisha and sneak away."

I went back inside with Kekoa, Cam, and Bunny, who opted to watch a movie in the media room. Once they were settled I headed to my room to grab my backpack. On my way there I noticed that the door to Ivan's office was cracked open just a bit. I could hear people talking inside, but I couldn't make out what they were saying. I hid behind a bookcase in the hallway and waited for them to emerge. It was Damien and Drusilla. She was carrying a large leather-bound book and paused, looking in my direction. I held my breath as I flattened myself against the wall. I wasn't all that well hidden and was sure she had seen me, but apparently she hadn't because she simply smiled and said something to Damien, who was carrying a wooden box with a lid that seemed to be locked.

Drusilla handed Damien the book she held and then returned to the office while he waited in the hall. When she came out again she had an additional book nestled in one arm as she closed the door behind her. The couple exchanged a few words before they headed toward the locked door that led to the east wing of the castle. I followed them as quietly as I could so as not to be noticed. When they got to the door Damien accessed a key panel behind a hidden door. He punched in a code and the door slid open. They went through and the door closed.

So the key to the other wings of the castle was a code. Now all I needed to do was figure out that code. I was willing to bet it would have something to do with Ivan's mother: her name, the day of her birth, the day of her death. I was pretty sure Buck would know the answers to at least some of those questions.

As I passed by the office I tried the knob. It was unlocked. Happy oversight or clever trap? I hesitated. Could Dru have seen me lurking outside the office and left the door unlocked hoping I'd go in or had she simply neglected to make certain the lock had caught? There was only one way to find out. I opened the door and silently slipped inside. The light was off and I was hesitant to turn it on for fear of being discovered, so I waited until my eyes adjusted to the darkness, then used the dim glow provided by a light on the computer hard drive to make my way over to the desk.

The desk drawers were locked, which wasn't surprising, but the computer was on, although the monitor was dark. I looked around the room a final time. If there were security cameras, as we all suspected, I'd be busted for sure, but I'd come this far; there was no way I was leaving until I saw what was on the screen.

I clicked the button on the front of the monitor and gasped when it came on. On the screen was a news article written five years before detailing the facts surrounding the case of a missing woman. She'd been reported missing by a friend who'd told the police she hadn't shown up for a charity event they were supposed to co-host. After an extensive search the woman was found in a shallow grave in an old cemetery that hadn't seen any new burials in almost a century. There were strange symbols carved into her skin that I realized matched the ones on the body of Ivan's former wife. The article referred to another death in which a victim had similar markings two years before that. It was believed both murders had taken place on Halloween night.

I heard a noise in the hall and quickly turned off the monitor. I prayed it wasn't Ivan as I slid down behind the desk. I held my breath as the door opened. Someone stepped into the room and took several steps inside. The light clicked on. I sank as close to the ground as I could, hoping I couldn't be seen from my hiding place. Someone else came into the room and stood behind the first person.

"See," the second person, whose voice sounded like Drusilla's, said. "I told you it was fine. You're getting as paranoid as Ivan."

"I swore I heard something in here."

"Let's go. You know Ivan doesn't like to be kept waiting. And grab that crystal. We might need it."

Both Drusilla and the first person, who I assumed was Damien, turned off the light and left the room, locking the door after them. I waited for several minutes to be sure they weren't still around before leaving my hiding space and tiptoeing to the door. I opened it a crack and, when the coast looked to be clear, slid into the hall, closing the door behind me.

I quickly ran upstairs and grabbed my backpack. As I filled it with the items we'd need for our hike I realized I should have taken another minute in the office to see if I could get Internet access. A quick e-mail to my cop brothers back on Oahu would go a long way toward increasing my comfort level. I stopped by the office on my way back out of the house, but as I thought it would be, the door was firmly locked.

"What took you so long?" Luke asked. "I was getting worried."

"Drusilla and Damien were in Ivan's office. They took out a couple of books and a wooden box. After they left I followed them to the door leading to the east wing and found out there's a key code lock on the door."

"Probably his mom's name," Cory said.

"That's exactly what I was thinking. Anyway, the key code isn't the most interesting thing I found." I glanced at Crystal before looking at Buck. Now that I'd started to speak I wasn't sure whether I should continue.

"Go on," Buck said. "What did you find?"

"Dru and Damien left the door to the office unlocked. I slipped inside and looked at Ivan's computer. When I turned on the monitor there was a news article about a woman who had been murdered and dumped in an old burial site. When her body was recovered they found it had been carved up with strange symbols."

"A ritual murder," Buck concluded.

"It would seem so. The murder took place five years ago and the article said that a similar murder had taken place two years before that."

"Both on Halloween?" Crystal guessed.

"It seems likely."

"So we have similar murders nine years ago, seven years ago, and five years ago," Crystal stated.

"Nine years ago?" Buck asked.

Crystal looked at me. I shrugged. It was her secret to tell or not.

"Cory and I found a newspaper article about a woman who'd been murdered in a similar style nine years ago," Crystal said.

"And we're thinking all three are related," Buck concluded.

"It seems they must be."

"Okay, hang on," Luke interrupted. "Drusilla and Damien are in the office and accidentally leave the door unlocked. You sneak in and there's a newspaper article about two killings that just happened to have been downloaded and is on the screen? That seems rather..."

"Staged," I completed. "Do you think we're intentionally being led on a wild-goose chase?"

"I don't know," Luke said.

"We still need to get out of here. Let's go look for that boat or helicopter," I suggested. "Does anyone even know how to fly a helicopter?"

"I do," Buck answered.

"Good. Now all we need to do is find one, free Tisha, and get the heck out of here."

The five of us decided the best way to look for a means of transportation was to hike to the top of the mountain in the middle of the island to see if we could get a view of the entire coastline from there. It was a huge island, so the odds of actually finding a boat or helicopter were slim, but we had to try something, and getting a feel for the terrain as a whole would be a start. The trail had dried since Luke and I had been out hiking and we'd gotten an early start; hopefully we'd find something before it got dark.

The trek became hot and uncomfortable, but we were making good progress and I predicted we'd reach the summit before noon. I thought I had a feel for the layout of the island that had been pieced together by conversations I'd had, combined with what I'd been able to observe on our journey to the island, along with the shorter treks Luke and I had taken, though I still couldn't reason where a boat might be docked if it wasn't where we'd been dropped off when we first arrived. There had to be a second cove or inlet that would provide protection from the storms that frequented the islands.

It was just a little after noon when we reached the summit. We'd been correct in assuming that location would provide us with a bird's-eye view of the whole island. We were easily able to identify the cove where we'd first docked, on the north side of the island. On either side of the cove was a rocky coastline unsuitable for docking. A good part of the rest of the coastline was rocky, although there was a small cove on the west side that appeared both clear and deep enough to accommodate a large private vessel. We didn't see a boat, but there was an odd grouping of greenery that looked almost as if it had been placed there strategically. My guess was that the trees had been planted to hide the location of a building that might be used to house a boat, possibly even a helicopter, from anyone who happened to fly overhead.

"Who is this guy and what's with all the secrecy?" I said aloud.

"It looks like there's someone down there," Crystal said, pointing.

Sure enough, I saw two men who were too far away to be identified, though neither was wearing black, so I assumed they worked for Ivan and weren't part of his Goth pack.

"So what now?" Cory asked. "Do we check out the location to see what exactly they're hiding or do we head back to the house?"

"I say we check it out," Crystal answered.

"Yeah, I'm for checking it out as well," I answered. "I wonder if there's an easier way of getting over there than going back the way we came and taking the beach west, though."

All five of us walked around the area, trying to map out the most logical route without getting lost. The jungle was dense and it would be difficult to make our way through if we didn't have a clearly marked trail to follow.

"What is that over there?" Luke pointed south, where an area had been cleared as if to plant a crop of some sort.

"I bet that's where the coffee bushes were planted," I answered. "Lazarus did say there were areas on the island where the plants still grew."

"Yeah, that makes sense."

Buck pointed to several dilapidated buildings. "Those must be left from when the island was a coffee plantation. If those structures were used to house farm workers it makes sense there would be a trail to the closest water, which would be the cove we're trying to reach. I bet if we can make our way to them we'll find a trail to the water."

"Okay," I said to Buck, "that makes sense, but how do we get to the buildings without a trail? Once we leave this mountaintop and hit the jungle we won't be able to see them until we find the clearing."

Buck pulled out a compass. Of course: a compass. Why didn't I think of that? I'd used a compass to navigate underwater when I was diving. I didn't have one with me now, but Buck had been in the army—and probably the Boy Scouts too—and carried one on his key chain.

The trek to the buildings was long and hot and buggy. There were several times when the jungle was so dense that I was certain we'd never find our way out, but Buck assured us he was on it, and sure enough, after a couple of hours of hiking we came out into the clearing just feet away from the closest building.

There was a small freshwater pool that we used to cool off before we continued on. I hoped the air was cooler at the coast; it was miserably hot in the interior of the island that day. It took a bit of doing, but eventually we found a trail that based on Buck's compass reading should take us to the water's edge. We'd need to hurry; we still needed to check out the hidden structure and hopefully make it back to the castle before nightfall. Luckily, the trail from the clearing to the water was much easier to navigate than the lack of trail through the jungle had been.

We stopped to figure out a plan to access what we believed was a hidden building when we got close enough to see the greenery that had caught my eye in the first place. There was no reason to believe the two men we'd seen from the mountaintop weren't still nearby.

"One of us should sneak down to see what's there," I suggested.

"It's too dangerous to go alone," Luke cautioned.

"It'll be harder to be stealthy with a large group," I argued.

"I'll go," Buck volunteered.

He seemed to know what he was doing, but he was quite a bit older than the rest of us and he had a wife to think about.

"No," I countered. "If there's a helicopter and whoever goes gets caught we'll need you to use it to go for help. I'll go."

"I'm going with you," Luke insisted.

"All right. I don't see the men, but if they come back and are heading toward us, create a diversion."

"How?" Crystal asked.

"Make some noise that will send them to investigate an area away from the orchard, but don't get caught."

"I'll take good care of them," Buck promised. "Keep your heads down and watch your backs."

Luke and I used the cover of the jungle to slowly make our way to the grove. As we got closer, we could clearly see that we'd been correct: The grove of quick-growing trees had been planted to camouflage a large building. I didn't see anyone around and I didn't hear any voices, but I wasn't dumb enough to think the men had simply left.

We slowly crept toward the entrance, trying desperately not to make any noise. My heart beat just a little bit harder with each snap of a twig or rustle in the underbrush. I stood perfectly still and listened for voices every few steps. I could feel Luke's presence behind me, but I didn't dare speak to him, so I stayed focused and continued on.

Sweat was dripping from my face and trailing down my back, but I barely noticed as I focused on the task at hand. It took some doing, but eventually we made it to the back of the building. There wasn't an entrance at the back, so we moved along until we came to a small door on the side. I slowly opened the door and peeked inside.

"Well, I'll be. I think we might have a bigger problem than we anticipated."

"Do you think we should take a closer look?"

Stacked in the building were rows and rows of wooden boxes. I looked around. I didn't see the men, but the door wasn't locked and I still doubted they'd simply left the area.

"I'll sneak in and take a peek; you watch my back. That way if I get caught you can alert the others."

I could see Luke was about to argue, so I scooted inside the building, removing his opportunity to do so. I tried to open the first box I came to, but it was nailed shut.

I had a pocket knife in my backpack; too bad I'd left it with the others.

I looked around the building for something to use. There was a workbench near a pair of large doors that looked as if they rolled up for loading and unloading. I'd need to expose my presence in order to reach them, so I debated what to do. I should probably just return to Luke to see if he had something we could use to pry open a box, but if he didn't I'd waste precious time. I decided to try to make my way toward the bench. If I stayed low and used the cover of the boxes I could make my way to within ten feet of it.

It took every ounce of self-control I had not to just make a run for the bench, but I knew it was wiser to stay hidden for as long as possible and slowly crawled around the building toward the front. When I got closer I noticed something else in front of the door: coffins. Two of them. I wondered if they were empty or occupied. I knew I needed to find something to open the wooden boxes and then get out of there, but my curiosity had been piqued and I found myself obsessing on the coffins. I changed direction and headed in their direction despite the fact that they were in an area of the building that would leave me totally exposed. I was about to open the lid on the first one when I heard voices. Someone was preparing to open the roll-up doors. As they began to rise, creating a sliver of light, I opened the first coffin and rolled inside.

Fortunately for me, it was empty.

"What are we supposed to do with these?" one of the men asked.

"Boss said they're going out with the next shipment."

"I've been tripping over them since they've been here. Do you think we should move them?"

"Guess we can move them back a bit."

I held my breath. If the *them* they wanted to move were the coffins, they were going to notice the unexpected heaviness of one of them, even though I barely weighed a hundred pounds.

I listened as both men approached. I knew they were standing only inches from me now. I was trying to decide what to do when I was discovered when one of them said, "On second thought, the boss did personally have the coffins placed here. Maybe it's best to leave them be. Boss said the boat will be here in two days, and I wouldn't want to end up being the body he's trying to dispose of."

"Yeah, me neither. It's hot today. I think I'll head over to the dock to take a swim."

"Best leave your phone behind. The boss is going to kill you for sure if you go for a swim with another phone in your pocket."

I listened as both men left the building. After I was certain they were gone I slowly lifted the lid to the casket and crawled out. I hurried over to the workbench, where I found both the phone and a screwdriver. I picked up the phone and looked at it. It wasn't a typical cell phone. I wondered if it was more of a walkie-talkie that only allowed you to communicate with others who had similar devices. I put it in my pocket and hurried over to where the boxes were stacked.

Oh, my. It was even worse than I'd thought.

Chapter 10

"So?" Crystal asked as soon as Luke and I returned.

"We didn't find a boat or a helicopter, but we did find something else."

"Such as?" Cory prompted.

"Boxes. Stacks and stacks of boxes."

Everyone looked confused for a minute before the light went on in Buck's mind and he said, "Drugs. You think Ivan is smuggling drugs?"

"Worse."

"What's worse than drugs?" Crystal asked.

"Guns. Big ones. Boxes and boxes of guns."

"Do you think we can use the guns to force Ivan to let us leave?" Crystal asked.

"I only opened one of the boxes, but I didn't notice any ammunition. Besides, I think creating a situation that could lead to a bloodbath doesn't seem like a really good plan."

"I guess that's true," Crystal conceded.

"In addition to the guns there are two coffins near the loading bay. They're empty. At least one of them is for sure; I didn't actually check the second one. The men we saw earlier were talking and I heard one of them say something about disposing of bodies."

Everyone looked just a bit paler after that statement.

"What now?" Crystal asked.

"I don't know," I admitted. Without a means of transportation I had no idea if we'd get off this island in one piece, and as odd as it sounded, I felt it was bad luck to say that out loud.

"Lani found this," Luke said. He took out the phone I'd taken from the bench and given to him for safekeeping.

"So we can call someone." Crystal smiled.

"It looks like this phone is set up for communication with a base phone only, not for communication in general, so I don't think we can use it, but it *is* a satellite phone, which leads me to believe the satellite signal that seems to be blocked on the rest of the island isn't blocked down by the beach. My own phone was in Lani's backpack, so I had to come back for it, but now that I have it Lani and I are going to go back to try to get out a call or at least a text to her brother. We won't be long, and when we come back we'll begin to work on plan B."

I could see the others were getting discouraged. *I* was getting discouraged. But we were doing what we could and in the end that would have to be enough.

Luke and I decided to return the walkie-talkie to the bench to keep from alerting the two men that there was anyone in the area. There was still no sign of them, but I had no doubt they were around, so we continued to sneak around in a stealthy manner. As soon as I dropped off the walkie-talkie, we tried to use Luke's phone on the beach, but all we could get was a weak signal. A call wouldn't go through, so I sent a text to my brother Jason of the Honolulu Police Department, hoping for the best.

"Sometimes texts go through when voice calls won't," Luke said in an attempt, I was certain, to cheer me up.

"Yeah. I guess we've done what we can. Let's head back."

By the time Luke and I rejoined the others they'd decided we should head back to the castle. We hadn't found a boat or helicopter as we'd hoped, and while it made sense to keep looking, we didn't want to be in the jungle after dark. Maybe Jason would get the text and come to our rescue. If not, I was sure we'd figure out something that would allow us to get everyone off the island in one piece.

The sun had set by the time we returned to the castle. Cam, Kekoa, and Bunny were happy to see us; they were beginning to worry. It had been several hours since I'd sent my SOS to Jason. If he'd received it, he would have been here by now; I'd estimated it wouldn't take him longer than ninety minutes to reach the island with his police boat, even less with a helicopter, if he started out right away. Chances were the text hadn't gone through.

After I showered and changed I headed downstairs to meet the others. We decided to grab sandwiches and take them out by the pool, where we felt we could talk. Our plan to find a mode of transportation to flee the island had failed; we desperately needed to come up with a new plan.

When I went into the kitchen to make up a plate I found Crystal alone. "I think given the circumstances we should fill Buck and Bunny in on everything," I said.

"I've been thinking about that," Crystal responded. "It does seem like Buck is trying to help us, and Bunny seems harmless enough. At this point we can use all the help we can get. Tomorrow is Halloween. We're running out of time."

I hugged Crystal. "I know you're worried. I am too. But we'll figure this out."

"I hope so. Maybe if we tell Buck and Bunny about Gwyneth they'll provide some new insights. Who knows; maybe they'll know something that makes sense of this whole thing."

Crystal and I joined the others and she shared the story of Ivan's first wife with Buck and Bunny. He frowned as he looked at the photo of Ivan Morningstar.

"Yeah, that's Ivan. He did have blond hair when he was younger. When I saw him this trip I just assumed he'd dyed it to fit in with the Goth theme. His eyes are blue, so he's wearing dark contacts as well." Buck looked at Crystal. "You think Ivan killed his wife and plans to kill your sister?"

"I suspected that when I first arrived on the island and now I feel certain of it. We need to get her away."

"Are we thinking the two dead women in the article Lani found are somehow related to all this?" Bunny asked.

"They do fit a pattern," Luke commented. "Gwyneth was killed nine years ago and the woman in the article was killed four years after that. The other body with similar marks on it mentioned in the news article was found two years prior to that. That makes murders nine, seven, and five years ago."

"I wonder if there were others?" I mused. "If the pattern is a murder every other year, there should have been one three years ago and another last year."

"If all the murders happened in odd-numbered years maybe we're safe now," Bunny contributed.

"If the pattern is to marry on even-numbered years and kill on odd-numbered ones, then this is a marrying year," Crystal agreed. "But even if that's true, Ivan plans to marry my sister this year and kill her next year."

"You think Ivan was married to all these women?" Buck asked.

Crystal looked at me. "Did the article you read mention whether the women who died were married and, if so, who they were married to?"

"I only read the first paragraph before the others came back, so I don't know what else the article said."

"I can probably pick the lock to the office," Cory volunteered.

"Everyone has been sequestered today; maybe the article is still on the screen," Crystal added.

"What about the cameras?" Kekoa asked.

"We need to find out what's going on. I think it's worth the risk." I looked at Cory. "If you can get the door open I'll go in."

Cory managed to get the door open and I snuck in while the others waited outside to keep an eye on things just in case someone came by. It didn't appear anyone had come into the office since I'd been in there that morning. The article was, indeed, still up on the screen.

The article had been written about the woman who'd died five years earlier. I reread it from the beginning. She'd been reported missing by a friend who'd told the police she hadn't shown up for a charity event. After an extensive search her body was found in a shallow grave in an old cemetery. I reread the information about the strange symbols carved into her skin, which I'd realized matched the ones on the body of Gwyneth Morningstar and the similar markings on another body two years earlier. While one murder had occurred in Los Angeles and the other in New York, the MEs were relatively certain both had taken place on Halloween night.

The article also said both women had been murdered on their first wedding anniversaries and speculated that the two events could be linked, though as of the date the article was published there was no proof to support the theory.

The woman who was murdered five years earlier had been married to a man named Blake Collins. There was no photo of either Blake or the victim herself. Could Blake Collins be Tisha's Ivan? There wasn't a lot of information about the woman who had been killed two years before that except to compare the marks on the bodies and that both women had been killed on Halloween night.

I was considering whether to look around some more when I heard Crystal's voice from just outside the office. She seemed to be speaking louder than was required in a normal conversation and it didn't take me long to figure out why. "Drusilla, what are you doing here? We were told all of you would be sequestered for the entire day."

"I just needed to get something from the office. It's best if you don't loiter out here. Ivan wouldn't like it."

"You know, I was just thinking about taking a swim. It's a lovely night out. Perhaps you could join us."

"Maybe another time."

Once again I hid under the desk.

The door opened and Drusilla came in. She walked directly to the desk without turning on the light. I was hiding just inches from where she stood and was sure she'd see me. She logged onto the computer and began to speak, although I wasn't aware of anyone else in the room.

"Meet me at the mausoleum at eleven. Come alone."

Then Drusilla left the room.

I waited several seconds before I crawled out from under the desk. I clicked on the monitor. The article was gone, the screen blank. I slowly made my way across the room and was about to peek out when the door opened. It was Luke and Cory.

"Are you okay?" Luke asked.

"Yeah. Let's go outside and I'll fill you in."

We joined the others, who were gathered around a table near the pool. Kekoa jumped up and hugged me. "Thank God," she said. "I was so scared when Drusilla showed up. I thought she'd find you for sure."

"I think she's trying to help us."

Pretty much everyone looked stunned.

"I don't know this for sure, but her movements seemed calculated. Like she wanted to help us stop whatever's going to happen, but she knows the castle has eyes and ears."

"What do you mean?" Cam asked.

"This morning when I was going up to get my backpack I saw Dru and Damien. I hid behind the bookcase, but I could swear she looked right at me. She paused and made an excuse to go back into the office before returning and leaving with Damien. When we spoke earlier we thought it a bit too convenient that the door was left unlocked and the article was already up on the computer screen. I think Dru did both of those things intentionally. Tonight, when she came into the office and I was hidden under the desk, she walked straight over to where I was without turning on the light. She stood at the computer and began to speak, although she never acknowledged my presence. She said to meet her at the mausoleum at eleven and to come alone."

"It sounds like a trap," Kekoa said.

"Maybe, but my gut is telling me otherwise. Something strange is going on; we all think so. I can't claim to know exactly what Ivan's plan is, but I'm worried that one or more people are meant to die."

"Tisha," Crystal said.

"No, I don't think so. Before Dru showed up I had time to read through the article. The woman who was killed five years ago was married to a man named Blake Collins. They'd been married exactly a year. There was no photo with the article, but it made sense to me that Blake and Ivan could be the same person. If that's true Ivan marries his women on even numbered years and kills them on odd numbered years. This is a marrying year."

"It does make it sound as if Ivan is a serial killer. You would think that would have been in the news," Buck pointed out.

"I don't have all the facts, but it looks like the killings all took place in different states and the husbands had slightly different names. The only link on the surface is the similar markings, which didn't seem to be noticed until the death five years ago. Without speaking to the investigators or having the opportunity to do further research it's hard to tell why the killer was never caught."

"Okay, back to Dru trying to help us," Luke interrupted. "Are we sure she isn't the killer? She's the one who told us to go to the mausoleum."

"Where we found Cam and Kekoa in time to help them. If she was the one who put them there or the one who shot Dharma, it makes no sense she'd send us to the exact location where she stashed the bodies. The only thing that does make sense is that Dru knows what's going on and doesn't know how to stop it. My theory is that Tisha invited us to the wedding without telling anyone so no one could stop her. Ivan either doesn't want to call undo attention to the event or perhaps needs Tisha to marry him voluntarily, so he didn't cancel our invitations. Dru could have seen our presence as her opportunity to intercede in whatever's going on without having to become personally involved."

"Dru was the only one of the Goth friends to meet us at the boat dock and come to the island with us," Kekoa acknowledged.

"Maybe she wanted to be sure we showed up," Cam added.

"I don't know." Buck sounded doubtful. "It doesn't track that Drusilla would be helping us. It almost seems like she's watching and manipulating us. It did appear she wanted you to go to the mausoleum so she sent you there, and it seems she wanted you to see the article so she had it downloaded on the computer and left the door open so you'd find it. I wouldn't interpret that as helping us until we can identify motive. I agree with Kekoa; I'd proceed with caution."

We all fell silent as each of us tried to figure out how to proceed. The waters were murky, that was for certain. I felt like I was trying to navigate a path I couldn't actually see.

"I guess at this point we have a choice to make," I eventually said. "Drusilla said to meet her. Do I go or not?"

"It's my sister's life we're talking about. I say we all go," Crystal voted.

"It sounds too dangerous." Bunny shook her head.

"She said to come alone," I reminded them.

"Are we forgetting about the it's-a-trap possibility?" Kekoa asked.

"I agree that it sounds like a trap." Cory glanced at Crystal with an apologetic look on his face.

"I vote no," Cam said. "We have no reason to trust that woman. For all you know, she could be luring you to the mausoleum to kill you."

I glanced at Buck, who had yet to speak. He shrugged. "I've walked into a lot dicier situations with a lot less intel. It seems that woman is reaching out to you, so I guess it's your decision."

I noticed Luke still hadn't commented. I looked directly at him. "What do you think?"

"I agree it may very well be a trap, but it's equally likely it isn't and Drusilla is trying to help us. You're the one who was asked to go, so I think it's up to you. But if you do go you aren't going alone."

"She said to meet her at eleven alone."

Luke looked at his watch. It was a quarter after ten. "Then I guess we'd better hurry."

Chapter 11

Luke had a good plan. He, along with Cory and Buck, hid in coffins while Cam waited with Kekoa, Crystal, and Bunny. The idea was for me to *go* alone to the meet but not to actually *be* alone. I had to admit I felt a lot better knowing the three men were hidden just out of sight. I intentionally arrived a few minutes early so I would already be there when Dru arrived so she wouldn't have time to look around.

"You came." Dru sounded surprised when she walked into the dark mausoleum.

"I wasn't sure I should, but I'm interested in finding out why you've been helping us."

Drusilla had a small flashlight that she shone around the building, I imagine to make certain we really were alone. "I don't have a lot of time, so I'll need to be brief. I'm not sure I'll be able to slip away again after this."

"Okay. I'm listening."

"My sister married Ivan a year ago."

I could see where this was going, but I just listened.

"I didn't attend the wedding nor had I ever met him, but Joslyn sent me a photo and a chatty letter from Paris, where they'd gone on their honeymoon. I was happy for her but a little put out that she'd gotten married without asking me to be there, but she said they'd eloped on the spur of the moment and she'd invite me to the island to meet her new husband when she got back. She never did."

"She never returned or she never invited you to meet her husband?"

"As far as I know, neither. The last correspondence I had from her was two months after she'd married, just a quick postcard from Greece, letting me know they had extended their honeymoon. There was no return address and she'd given up her cell phone, so I had no way to get hold of her. We've always been close. Really close. It made no sense that she would just disappear like that."

"So you began to investigate?"

Drusilla nodded. "I didn't have a lot to go on, but I noticed that in the photo she sent me from Paris Joslyn had a new tattoo on her neck that seemed very unlike anything she would be interested in getting. It took weeks of searching, but I eventually stumbled across the article I had waiting for you to find on the computer when you snuck into the office, as I was sure you would. The tattoo my sister had matched one of the symbols carved on the dead woman exactly. The more I thought about it, the more I realized small details my sister had mentioned in her letter that hadn't registered at the time suddenly seemed significant."

"What kind of things?"

"Little things, like that they'd gotten married on the thirty-first, and I realized she was referring to October thirty-first, Halloween. She also said her husband's name was Ivan and that he owned a private island on Hawaii with a real castle on it. When I started to put everything together I realized Joslyn might very well be caught up in the same thing the other women who had died had become."

"So what did you do?"

"I found out exactly which island my sister's husband owned, borrowed a small boat, and snuck onto it to look around. I didn't find Joslyn, but I did notice that pretty much everyone on the island was dressed in black and sported tattoos and piercings. I decided the best way to find my sister was from the inside, so I bought a bunch of black leather, got a few tattoos and several visible piercings, and started looking for a way in. Quite by chance I met Damien six months ago, when he came to Oahu with some of the others for supplies. He told me that he lived on the island, and I made a point of gaining his interest. He brought me here and introduced me as Drusilla, and no one was any the wiser that my real name was Heather."

"And your sister?"

"I've never found her. I'm pretty sure she's dead, but I have no proof. The man Joslyn told me she was married to was engaged to someone else by that time, and none of the others remembered anyone fitting my sister's description, although I had to be careful about coming right out and asking whether Ivan had been married before. Still, I'm pretty sure he never brought my sister to this island, or if he did it was only for a short time and he kept her isolated."

"So you cozied up to Morticia to see what you could find out?"

"Exactly. I quickly discovered she was more of a pawn than anything else. Ivan was clearly in charge, and Lazarus seems to be his right-hand man with a lot of power of his own. There are actually quite a few people living in the castle, minions mostly. People you've never met and likely never will. In fact, Ivan has only seen fit to introduce you to his inner circle."

"And you're part of this inner circle?"

"I am now. I knew my way into the inner circle was through Morticia, so I made a point of befriending her. The others don't seem to have much use for Ivan's current love interest, so it was actually pretty easy to achieve the title of best friend. She asked me to attend her wedding and I enthusiastically accepted. At first she seemed to have the run of the island, but as the wedding got closer Ivan began keeping a closer eye on her. I haven't had any time alone with her in the past month."

"Does she know why you're really here?"

"No. In the beginning I didn't think I could trust her. She was, after all, engaged to the man I suspected of killing my sister. By the time I figured out she was most likely Ivan's next victim, he'd already sequestered her in his tower."

"What about when we were dress shopping? It was just us. You could have said something then."

"It wasn't just us. Two of Ivan's minions were following us the entire day.

They weren't dressed in Goth garb, so you probably didn't notice the two women who shadowed our every move."

"Your story sounds reasonable and I guess I believe you, but why did you ask me here tonight?"

"Something is about to happen. I'm not sure what, but I have a feeling someone is going to die. Probably tonight. I don't think it's Morticia, but Ivan and Lazarus have been acting strange. Dharma seemed to think you were the one to help us, so I'm asking."

"Dharma? You know she's dead, right?"

"No, I don't think so, although I'm not sure she's alive either."

"Huh?"

"Dharma came to me a couple of weeks after I arrived on the island. I was down on the beach and she just appeared. I thought she was a hallucination at first. She seemed to talk in circles and she popped in and out in such a way that I was left questioning whether she was actually there or not, but eventually I realized she was here to help me. All I want at this point is to find out for certain whether my sister is alive or dead and then get off this island in one piece."

"But the others can see her?"

"Yeah. Everyone seems to know who Dharma and Oz are, although they're rarely around. One of the women who hangs out here told me they were already on the island when Ivan bought it, and while she didn't know where they lived, she said she believed they just never left after it was sold to Ivan."

I supposed that made sense. If they knew the island intimately that would explain how they seemed to pop in and out. Anyone who had lived here their entire lives would know all the trails and shortcuts.

"What is it you want me to do?"

Dru looked around. "I have to go. There's a ceremony that's going to take place in the sacred room at midnight. The room is at the end of the hallway you saw Damien and me go through today. The code is 103105."

Drusilla ran for the door and was gone.

"What do you think?" I asked.

Luke, Cory, and Buck all raised the lids of the coffins in which they were hiding and climbed out.

"I still think it could be a trap," Buck offered.

"I agree," Luke seconded. "Besides, her story about the sister doesn't fit the pattern. Hadn't we already decided that

Ivan married during even-numbered years and killed on odd-numbered ones? If he married her sister last year it was during a killing year."

"I suppose you could be right and it is a trap. Maybe Dru didn't figure out the pattern and didn't know there was a flaw in her story, but if it's not a trap and she is who she says she is, crashing the ceremony might be our best chance to stop whatever is going to happen," Cory said.

"Let's go back to the castle and let the others know what's going on," I suggested. "If I know Kekoa she's getting worried right about now."

When we returned we gathered around the pool to discuss the situation. If we were going to try to sneak in to find out what the ceremony was all about we only had a few minutes to come up with a plan.

We'd just settled down when all the lights went out. I realized if the power was out the electronic door wouldn't work and this conversation might be for naught. Several seconds later the power came back on and we continued our conversation.

"So do we agree that a few of us will at the very least check things out?" I asked.

"I don't like it," Kekoa restated her opinion for the tenth time since we'd begun our discussion. "If it talks like a trap and walks like a trap it's probably a trap."

"A trap to what end?" I asked.

"Maybe Drusilla wants you to go to the ceremony so they can capture you and sacrifice you to whatever demon they worship."

"We're pretty much helpless on this island. If Ivan means any of us harm I don't know that there's much we can do about it. I'm sure he knows that as well as we do. I don't think he needs a trap if his intention is to sacrifice any of us, so maybe Dru is who she says she is and she really does just want us to stop whatever it is that's going to happen."

"I say we go," Crystal voted. "It might be our best chance to rescue Tisha."

"Rescue her and then what?" Bunny asked. "We still don't have a way off the island. Bringing attention to ourselves seems reckless."

"Bunny is right," Buck agreed. "Without a means of escape a rescue plan is fruitless."

"We at least need to know what they're up to," Crystal pleaded. "My sister's life is at stake."

I'm not sure how I became captain of this little team, but it felt like everyone was looking to me to make the decision. The problem was, I had no idea what to do. Those who pointed out that rescuing Tisha while we were all trapped on the island ourselves was pointless weren't wrong; still, I kept remembering Dharma's face when she said I was the one they were waiting for.

"I need to stop in the bathroom," I announced. "We're running out of time, so continue this discussion. I'll be right back."

I trotted back to the castle and immediately headed down the hallway Dru had instructed me to take. I knew it was my destiny to do something, even if I didn't know what that something was going to be, but I didn't want to put anyone else in danger. When I got to the keypad it was flashing on and off. I tried the code Drusilla had given me, but it didn't work. I supposed it could have been disrupted when the power went off and the door needed to be reset. I was trying to decide what to do when everything went black.

Waking up in a coffin is an odd experience, and one I never want to repeat. I remembered that the coffins didn't lock, but I could hear voices, so I decided it wouldn't be my best move to announce the fact that I'd regained consciousness. I wondered what had happened to the others. Surely they'd gone to look for me by now.

"What are we going to do with her?" a voice I was sure belonged to Lilith asked.

"It's up to the boss, but most likely we'll have to kill her along with the rest."

I wasn't sure who the second person was, but it wasn't Lazarus. I'd noticed he had a faint accent. And I didn't think it was Ivan, who had a deeper voice.

"There are people who know they came to the island. Killing them will bring attention we don't want," Lilith said.

"True," he agreed. "It seems they're suspicious of Ivan and his little fetish. Maybe we can pin this whole thing on him."

I could hear someone else enter the room. "Are they all accounted for?" I was pretty sure this third person was Lazarus.

"We have the nosy woman on ice and her friends are all locked up in the parlor. Damien is with them," Lilith told him.

"Raven is with Ivan and the women," the second person I'd heard speak, who I still couldn't identify, added. "It's her opinion that the sacrifice should continue as planned, but I'm not sure that's the best course of action. Maybe we should just load the merchandise onto the boat and take off before it's too late."

"I agree," Lazarus answered. "I'll take care of our prisoners while you see to the boat. I'll meet you at the dock in thirty minutes."

I listened as everyone seemed to leave the room, then waited a full two minutes to be sure no one had stayed behind before I gently pushed on the lid of the coffin. It didn't open. I pushed harder. It still didn't budge. I pushed with all my might. Nothing. Panic began to build when I realized the coffin I was in this time wasn't the same as the others. This one was secured from the outside, and no matter how hard I pushed, it wouldn't open. I started to hyperventilate as the darkness closed in around me. I'd never been afraid of either the dark or small spaces before, but suddenly I was terrified of both. I wanted to scream, but I knew there was no one to hear my cries, so instead I prayed.

I wondered how long I'd been there, and whether I was in the mausoleum or if I'd been taken to one of the wings of the castle that only those closest to Ivan seemed to have access to. After what seemed like hours but was probably only minutes the coffin opened and I took a deep breath of relief. "Oz! How did you know I was here?" I looked around the windowless room that was definitely not the mausoleum. "Where are we?"

"We don't have time to waste. Lazarus is going to kill the three women."

"I heard Lazarus with two others before they left the room? I think one was Lilith but I didn't recognize the voice of the other. They talked about killing people and pinning it on Ivan."

"Ivan is dead. Lazarus killed him. Come; we must hurry."

I moved after Oz, hoping he had a plan. He led me to a balcony that looked down on a room that was lit only with candles. In the center stood three women, all dressed in white. Dru and Tisha were two of them, but I didn't recognize the third. Lying next to them was Ivan, also dressed in white but covered with blood.

"I'm sorry, ladies," Lazarus said as he stood before them holding a scythe. "Killing his mother year after year was Ivan's thing and I truly wish you no harm, but things have spiraled out of control. I find I need to abandon my plans and head for the open sea."

"You don't have to kill us," Drusilla insisted. "We won't tell anyone about the guns."

"I'm afraid your nosy friends know too much. Killing you is my only way out. I'll simply tell everyone that Ivan killed you as part of a sacrifice and that I killed him in my attempt to save you. The others know of Ivan's particular fetish. They'll back me up if need be."

I screamed as Lazarus raised his scythe. He paused and looked at me. "Well, well. Look who's risen from the dead. And I thought that was my gig."

"I have a weapon," I bluffed.

"Really?" Lazarus took several steps toward me. I couldn't help but focus on his black eyes and my heart beat faster and faster as he climbed the steps to the balcony where I stood. "And what sort of a weapon might that be?"

I was about to try bluff number two when the door burst open and my brother Jason, along with five other armed men, came running into the room.

"Them," I said as I sank to the floor.

The police officers quickly restrained Lazarus, who didn't say anything as he was brought to the floor and cuffed.

"Are you okay?" Jason picked me up off the floor and hugged me tight.

"Yeah. How did you know I was in trouble?"

"I got your text. I came as fast as I could."

"The text? I sent that hours ago."

"I don't know what to tell you. It came through just over an hour ago."

I remembered the power outage. It had lasted only a few seconds, but it must have been long enough to allow whatever was blocking the satellite signal to go offline, which allowed the text, which was in queue, to finally send.

"And the others?"

"They're waiting on the patio."

I threw my arms around Jason and began to sob. "Let's go home."

Chapter 12

Monday, October 31

"I'd say you know how to celebrate Halloween better than anyone I've ever met," my friend Sean teased.

After I'd confirmed that Luke and everyone else was okay I'd let a uniformed officer take Cam, Kekoa, and me home while Jason stayed on the island to deal with the mess we'd left behind. We slept for much of the day but awoke just in time to attend the Halloween party our neighbors, Sean Trainor and Kevin Green, were having.

"Trust me, waking up locked in a coffin in Dracula's castle with no means of escape isn't the Halloween thrill you might think."

Sean hugged me before handing me a beer. "I'm just glad you and everyone else are okay."

"Me too."

I took my beer and settled into a chair on the lanai overlooking the ocean. It was good to be home with my friends, my dog, and my neighbors after the nightmare of the past few days. I watched the gentle waves roll one right after the other onto the beach. It was a warm night and a gently breeze carried the scent of flowers. I hadn't had time to fully process everything, mostly due, I was sure, to the fact that there was so much to think about.

As it turned out, Drusilla's sister Joslyn hadn't died in Europe as she'd feared. We still weren't certain exactly what had happened, but at some point after the killing five years earlier Ivan's timeline had been interrupted and he'd married Drusilla's—or I guess I should say Heather's—sister last year instead of two years ago. His plan, according to Damien, who'd squealed like a pig in an attempt to save his own butt once the HPD had secured the property, was to kill Heather's sister on the same night he married Tisha, which would once again restore order as far as he was concerned.

When Lazarus had figured out that Tisha's guests had found out about the guns he was selling on the black market, he'd realized he needed to move up his timeline before any of us had a chance to go to the cops. Lazarus had decided to kill

Ivan as well as all three women to make it appear like Ivan was behind everything that had been going on and had been killed when Lazarus tried to save the women.

Cole, who according to Damien, had been shot by Raven, was really dead. It seemed Raven and Damien had been having an affair; when Cole found out and threatened to tell Drusilla, Raven decided he'd become a liability. Damien didn't know what had actually happened to Dharma or whether she was alive or dead.

"Mind if I join you?" Luke asked as he sat down next to me.

"Did Buck and Bunny get off okay?" Luke had volunteered to drive them to the airport.

"They did, and Cory and Crystal have headed to Maui with Crystal's sister for a little rest and relaxation before they head home as well."

"I'm glad everything worked out okay, although I do wish I knew what happened to Oz and Dharma. I still don't know if Dharma was really dead or if the whole thing was staged."

"I'm not sure we're meant to know the answer to that, but if it would make you feel better I'll take you back to the island and we can look around after the police department is done with their investigation."

"Yeah, I might want to do that."

"As far as unsolved mysteries go, I did find out it was Damien who hit Cam and Kekoa over the head and put them in the coffins. Damien told the police that Ivan was on the beach with Lilith, who he'd been having an ongoing affair with, and Damien knew Ivan wouldn't want Cam and Kekoa to know he wasn't faithful to Tisha, so he knocked them out and stashed them in the coffins."

"Why'd he put them in the coffins?"

"I don't know. Maybe to make sure Ivan didn't find out about what had happened and kill them just to be safe. I don't think Damien is a particularly evil guy I think he just got caught up in a cultlike situation and didn't have the moral fiber to realize he should try to stop what was going on."

"Now that Ivan is dead I wonder what will be done with the island."

"I guess that depends on whether Ivan had a will. If not, I suppose Buck would be his next of kin. If he inherits the island he can do as he wishes with the property."

My dog Sandy came over and put his head in my lap. He'd barely left my side since I'd been home. I was sure my sister-in-law had taken good care of him while I was on the island, but he wasn't used to me being gone for so long.

"Did you find out what was going on with the guns Lazarus had?"

"Not specifically," Luke answered. "The HPD believes the guns were stolen or obtained on the black market and that Lazarus had a buyer lined up, most likely foreign, but they really don't have any specifics yet. If I had to guess, I'd say Ivan wasn't involved in the gun trade. Lazarus used the island as a way station and Ivan must have known what he was doing and let him. It seems Ivan was just a rich investor who used his money to play out his fantasies, which, it seems to me, all revolved around his mother."

"Yeah, Lazarus said something about Ivan killing his mother over and over again when I was in the coffin. I wonder if he killed her the first time."

Luke frowned, "What do you mean?"

"Buck said his mother died in her sleep. He also said she was obsessed with Ivan. It occurred to me that perhaps Ivan killed her in a fit of rage or to free himself from her hold and then felt guilty, which caused his need to kill her over and over again."

Luke grimaced. "This conversation is getting way too twisted for me. Do you want to go for a walk?"

I looked at Sandy. "How about it? Want to take a walk?"

He barked.

I turned to Luke. "We'd love to."

Luke stood up, took my hand, and pulled me to my feet. I glanced inside Sean and Kevin's condo. Cam and Kekoa were talking to our next-door neighbor, Elva, and it looked as if everyone was having a good time. Once again I said a prayer of thanks that the four of us had gotten off the island in one piece.

Luke and I walked hand in hand down the beach with Sandy running ahead of us. We didn't speak as we let the rhythm of the waves lull us into a sense of serene contentment. The moon was out to light our way as we walked farther and farther from the condo.

"My mother called me today," Luke eventually said.

"That's nice. How's your family?"

"They're doing well. My oldest sister is expecting another baby, which has Mom planning showers and christening gowns."

"It's nice your family is so close, like mine."

Luke stopped walking. He turned so that we were facing each other. "Mom wants me to come home for Christmas. The small town we live closest to does Christmas up big every year and she wants the whole family to attend the festivities."

I felt my heart sink. I understood why Luke would want to be with his family for the holiday, but I was going to miss him so much if he wasn't here. "Are you going to go?"

"I'm not sure yet."

"What about the horses?"

"I have people who can stay at the ranch and see to things. I miss my family and it would be nice to be home for Christmas, but I also want to spend Christmas with you. I thought about putting my mom off until next year, but Christmas is a day for families and I wasn't certain what your plans were, or if you'd even thought about spending Christmas with me."

I felt like I was standing face to face with one of those seemingly small moments that, when you looked back on them, turned out to be really big. I'd been simultaneously pulling Luke close and pushing him away for months. I knew what he was really asking was whether we were in the sort of relationship where we should assume we'd spend a day as important as Christmas together.

I looked into Luke's eyes as I considered my answer. I knew I was in love with him, but I was also afraid. I loved Hawaii and couldn't even begin to imagine living anywhere else. What if Luke tired of island living and moved back to Texas? I knew my heart would be ripped from my chest as I watched him walk away. Of course protecting my heart might be a thing of the past. Even if Luke left at this very moment my life would never be the same.

"Yes," I answered. "I have thought about Christmas and I do want to spend it with you." I stood on tiptoe and wrapped my arms around his neck. "This Christmas, next Christmas, every Christmas."

Luke lifted me off the ground and kissed me. It wasn't a kiss between friends and it wasn't a kiss of burning passion. It was a kiss of commitment. A kiss of promise.

"Come back to the ranch with me," he whispered against my lips.

I kissed him lightly before I replied. "Just give me a minute to grab a few things and tell the others."

Later, when I look back on that night, the night I fully committed my body and my soul to the displaced cowboy I still felt might break my heart, I would realize that somehow I knew, deep down inside, that life doesn't come with guarantees and we never really know how things will work out. As I think back on that night, I understand there are times when you need to close your eyes and take a blind leap of faith that life is fair and love prevails and, in the end, following your heart despite the risks works out infinitely better than playing it safe and missing all that love has to offer.

Recipes

Recipes from Kathi

Apple Pie Biscuits
Pumpkin Cookies
Carrot Cake
Cranberry Muffins

Recipes from Readers

Apple Cake – submitted by Pam Curran
Creeping Crust Cobbler – submitted by
Nancy Farris
Pumpkin Crumb Cake – submitted by
Jeanie Daniel
Banana Peach Bar Cookies – submitted by
Joanne Kocourek

Apple Pie Biscuits

Preheat oven to 375 degrees.
Spray a 6 x 9 baking dish on all sides with nonstick spray.
Open 1 can large buttermilk biscuits (I use Pillsbury Grands).
Melt 1 stick (½ cup) butter (I melt it in a bowl in the microwave).

Combine in a bowl:
½ cup white sugar
½ cup brown sugar
1 tsp. nutmeg
1 tbs. cinnamon

Dip each biscuit into butter coating on both sides. Then dip each biscuit into sugar mixture coating on both sides.
Place into baking dish.

Topping:
Top with 1 can of apple pie filling.
Combine remaining butter with remaining sugar mixture. Add ½ cup oatmeal and 1

cup chopped pecans. Pour over top of biscuits.

Bake at 375 degrees for 35 minutes.

Pumpkin Cookies

Cream together:
1 cube margarine, softened
½ cup sugar

Add and mix thoroughly:
½ cup dark corn syrup
1 cup canned pumpkin
1 egg beaten
1 tsp. vanilla

Add to pumpkin mixture and mix
thoroughly:
2 cups flour
1 tsp. baking soda
½ tsp. salt
1 tsp. vanilla

Stir in:
I cup chopped walnuts

Drop onto greased cookie sheet. Flatten
with fork.
Bake at 375 degrees for about 15 minutes
(or until browned).
Cool and frost.

Frosting:
¾ cup butter, softened
6 oz. cream cheese, softened
1 tbs. vanilla
3 cups powdered sugar

Carrot Cake

3 eggs
2 cups sugar
3 cups carrots, finely shredded
1 8-oz. pkg. cream cheese, softened
1¼ cup vegetable oil
2 cups flour
2 tbs. ground cinnamon
2 tsp. baking soda
1 tsp. salt
1 can 8-oz. crushed pineapple, well drained
2 cups walnuts, chopped

Beat eggs and sugar together until blended. Add carrots, cream cheese, and oil. Beat until smooth. Add dry ingredients. Stir in pineapple and nuts. Pour into greased 9 x 13 baking dish. Bake at 350 degrees for 55–60 minutes.

Frosting:
¾ cup butter, softened
6 oz. cream cheese, softened
1 tbs. vanilla
3 cups powdered sugar

Whip together; frost cake when cool and top with pecans.

Cranberry Muffins

Combine in large bowl:

2 cups flour
1 cup sugar
1½ tsp. baking powder
1 tsp. ground nutmeg
1 tsp. ground cinnamon
½ tsp. ground ginger
½ tsp. baking soda
½ tsp. salt

Cut in:

1 stick butter

Add:

¾ cup orange juice
2 eggs, beaten
1 tbs. vanilla extract

Fold in:

1½ cups cranberries, chopped
2 cups pecans, chopped

Apple Cake

Submitted by Pam Curran

This fresh apple cake is from an old friend. Instead of the traditional
birthday cake, she made this for mine one year. And even gave me the
recipe to share.

3 large red apples, grated, with peel
2 cups sugar
Mix and let stand 20 minutes.

2½ cups flour
1 tsp. baking soda
½ tsp. salt
1 tsp. cinnamon
Mix and add to apple mixture by hand (no mixer). Then add:

1 cup vegetable oil
2 beaten eggs
1 tsp. vanilla

Add to flour mixture. Stir in 1 cup chopped nuts and ½ cup raisins, optional. Bake at 350 degrees for 1 hour or until golden brown. Let cool for 10 minutes before turning from pan. It can be frozen.

Makes 2 loaves.

Creeping Crust Cobbler

Submitted by Nancy Farris

This is a favorite of ours because it's so quick and delicious. It's based on a recipe my mother submitted to our church cookbook 30+ years ago.

¼ cup unsalted butter
1 cup flour
1 cup sugar
1 tsp. baking powder
½ tsp. salt
¾ cup milk
2 cups fresh or frozen fruit, sliced (cherries, berries, peaches—your choice)

Heat oven to 350 degrees.
Melt butter in 8" or 9" baking dish.
Mix dry ingredients together and stir in milk. Pour on top of melted butter. Place fruit on top. Bake for 30 minutes or until brown. If using frozen fruit, may need to add 5 minutes more.
While still warm, top with ice cream or whipped cream.

Pumpkin Crumb Cake

Submitted by Jeanie Daniel

This is a cake I threw together one day from ingredients I had on hand, and the grandkids now ask for it all the time.

1 yellow cake mix (any kind)
½ cup unsalted butter, melted
4 eggs
1 15-oz. can (2 cups) pumpkin
1 can evaporated milk
½ cup brown sugar
 2 tsp. cinnamon
½ cup sugar
½ cup unsalted butter, melted
Plus ¼ cup softened butter

Take out 1 cup of the cake mix and set aside. Mix remaining cake mix, melted butter, and 1 egg. Pat this mixture into the bottom of a 9 x 13 pan. Mix pumpkin, evaporated milk, brown sugar, cinnamon, and the remaining three eggs. Pour mixture over crust. Now mix reserved cake mix, ½ cup sugar, ¼ cup softened butter until crumbly and sprinkle over pumpkin mixture. Bake at 350 degrees for 1 hour. When cake is slightly cool, drizzle caramel ice cream sauce over the cake.

Banana Peach Bar Cookies

Submitted by: Joanne Kocourek

These cookies were created while we were staying at the Ronald McDonald House in Atlanta, GA, using family pantry items.

¼ cup butter, softened
½ cup sugar
1 cup peach preserves (divided into two ½ cup portions)
1 egg
½ tsp. vanilla
¼ cup chopped almonds

In mixing bowl, cream the butter and sugar until fluffy. Add the ½ cup preserves, egg, and vanilla to the creamed mixture; mix well.

⅔ cup all-purpose flour
¼ tsp. baking powder
¼ tsp. baking soda
⅛ tsp. salt
1 very ripe small banana, mashed (¼ cup)
½ cup flaked coconut

Thoroughly stir together the flour, baking powder, baking soda, and salt. Stir into creamed mixture. Blend in the mashed banana and coconut; mix well. Spread in greased 9 x 9-inch baking pan. Bake at 350 degrees until cookies test done, 23 to 25 minutes.

Spread warm cookies with the remaining ½ cup preserves. Sprinkle with the chopped almonds. Cool cookies thoroughly; cut into bars. Makes 24.

Note: Use peach preserves. Jelly does NOT work for this recipe.
This can be modified using pineapple or pineapple-orange preserves for a tropical-flavored bar cookie.

Books by Kathi Daley

Come for the murder, stay
for the romance.

Zoe Donovan Cozy Mystery:

Halloween Hijinks
The Trouble With Turkeys
Christmas Crazy
Cupid's Curse
Big Bunny Bump-off
Beach Blanket Barbie
Maui Madness
Derby Divas
Haunted Hamlet
Turkeys, Tuxes, and Tabbies
Christmas Cozy
Alaskan Alliance
Matrimony Meltdown
Soul Surrender
Heavenly Honeymoon
Hopscotch Homicide
Ghostly Graveyard
Santa Sleuth
Shamrock Shenanigans
Kitten Kaboodle
Costume Catastrophe
Candy Cane Caper – *October 2016*

Tj Jensen Paradise Lake Mysteries
Coming September 6, 2016, from Henery Press

Pumpkins in Paradise
Snowmen in Paradise
Bikinis in Paradise
Christmas in Paradise
Puppies in Paradise
Halloween in Paradise
Treasure in Paradise – *April 2017*

Whales and Tails Cozy Mystery:

Romeow and Juliet
The Mad Catter
Grimm's Furry Tail
Much Ado About Felines
Legend of Tabby Hollow
Cat of Christmas Past
A Tale of Two Tabbies
The Great Catsby
Count Catula – *September 2016*
Cat of Christmas Present – *November 2016*

Seacliff High Mystery:

The Secret
The Curse
The Relic
The Conspiracy
The Grudge

Sand and Sea Hawaiian Mystery:

Murder at Dolphin Bay
Murder at Sunrise Beach
Murder at the Witching Hour

Road to Christmas Romance:

Road to Christmas Past

Kathi Daley lives with her husband, kids, grandkids, and Bernese mountain dogs in beautiful Lake Tahoe. When she isn't writing, she likes to read (preferably at the beach or by the fire), cook (preferably something with chocolate or cheese), and garden (planting and planning, not weeding). She also enjoys spending time on the water when she's not hiking, biking, or snowshoeing the miles of desolate trails surrounding her home.

Kathi uses the mountain setting in which she lives, along with the animals (wild and domestic) that share her home, as inspiration for her cozy mysteries.

Kathi is a top 100 mystery writer for Amazon and she won the 2014 award for both Best Cozy Mystery Author and Best Cozy Mystery Series.

She currently writes four series: Zoe Donovan Cozy Mysteries, Whales and Tails Island Mysteries, Sand and Sea Hawaiian Mysteries, and Seacliff High Teen Mysteries.

Giveaway:

I do a giveaway for books, swag, and gift cards every week in my newsletter, *The Daley Weekly* http://eepurl.com/NRPDf

Other links to check out:
Kathi Daley Blog – publishes each Friday http://kathidaleyblog.com
Webpage – www.kathidaley.com
Facebook at Kathi Daley Books – www.facebook.com/kathidaleybooks
Kathi Daley Teen – www.facebook.com/kathidaleyteen
Kathi Daley Books Group Page – https://www.facebook.com/groups/569578823146850/
E-mail – kathidaley@kathidaley.com
Goodreads – https://www.goodreads.com/author/show/7278377.Kathi_Daley
Twitter at Kathi Daley@kathidaley – https://twitter.com/kathidaley
Amazon Author Page – https://www.amazon.com/author/kathidaley

BookBub –
https://www.bookbub.com/authors/
kathi-daley
Pinterest –
http://www.pinterest.com/kathidale
y/

61168924R00128

Made in the USA
Middletown, DE
08 January 2018